CRAWLSPACE

"The Lees Sisters, Lonni and Arlette, are unique; these two gals write their own work in their own way, but they always deliver sharp, exciting, intense crime stories you can really sink your teeth into. You can't go wrong with the stories in this book."

Gary Lovisi, *Hardboiled Magazine*

"When *Hardboiled Magazine* publishes new authors, I've learned over the years it's worth paying attention, and Lonni Lees is no exception. Her crime story, "The Blue-Eyed Bandit," merges a pitch perfect *Black Mask* pulp style with a more modern psychotic noir, with the result being that Ms. Lees is someone readers should be on the lookout for."

David Zeltserman, Author of *Small Crimes*

Nine dark tales of crime, crazies, and crawlspaces— bet you can't read just one!

Borgo Press Books by LONNI LEES

Crawlspace and Other Dark Stories
Deranged: A Novel of Horror

CRAWLSPACE

AND OTHER DARK STORIES

LONNI LEES

THE BORGO PRESS

MMXI

CRAWLSPACE

FIRST EDITION

Published by Wildside Press LLC

www.wildsidebooks.com

DEDICATION

For my husband, ***Jonathan DuHamel***, who is forever slaying the numerous evil gremlins that lurk in my computer, for his patience and invaluable assistance.

And for ***Gary Lovisi*** at *Hardboiled* magazine, for all of his support and encouragement along the way.

CONTENTS

INTRODUCTION

Deep beneath the surface, they hide in all of us. The crawl-spaces, cobwebbed basements, shadowed alleyways and musty attics of our minds; they are the dark and dangerous corners of the human psyche. Dormant, they lie in wait. Some pretend they're not there and go about their innocuous lives, while others grab hold and pull them to the surface, feeding on their dark forces. Whether a career criminal, a madman, a thug, an abused spouse or an innocent child, within these pages you'll find those who have embraced that darkness. Some tap into it for survival, some for greed. Some use it for destruction, some just because it's there. It dwells within all of us. Waiting.

—Lonni Lees

ACKNOWLEDGMENTS

THESE STORIES WERE previously published as follows, and are reprinted (with minor editing, updating, and textual modifications) by permission of the author:

"The Blue-Eyed Bandit" was originally published in *Hardboiled* #37, March 2008, and reprinted in *More Whodunits: The Second Borgo Press Book of Crime and Mystery Stories*, edited by Robert Reginald, Borgo Press, 2011. Copyright 2008, 2011 by Lonni Lees.

"Crawlspace" was originally published in *Hardboiled* #42, December 2010. Copyright 2010, 2011 by Lonni Lees.

"Dead Man's Dance" was originally published in *Yellow Mama* #18, February 15, 2010. Copyright 2010, 2011 by Lonni Lees.

"The One-Eyed Belly Dancer" was originally published in *Deadly Dames*, Bold Venture Press, 2009. Copyright 2009, 2011 by Lonni Lees.

"Tumbleweed" was originally published in *Hardboiled* #36, January 2007. Copyright 2007, 2011 by Lonni Lees.

"Irrefutable Evidence," "The Watercolor Witness," "Daddy's Girls," and "Possum" are published here for the first time. Copyright 2011 by Lonni Lees.

THE BLUE-EYED BANDIT

The hot wind blew. Dust smothered the afternoon sun to a grotesque twilight as the old '32 Ford sped down the highway between Ensign and Copeland. The dust bowl continued to wreak its devastation on this isolated corner of Kansas, annihilating lives and livelihoods, leaving nothing but ruin and broken dreams in its wake.

Frank Lanigan grumbled aloud as he floored the gas pedal, putting as much distance between himself and Ensign as he could. And as quickly as possible. He doubted he was being chased but wasn't taking chances. He hadn't become successful at his trade by being careless; but today something screwed up; blighted his stellar reputation. Now, in a split second, it was fucked.

Earlier that afternoon Frank had walked into the Ensign bank, Tommy gun held firmly in his grasp, empty black leather satchel tucked under one arm. He'd hit a good ten banks between Chicago and Kansas, an easy living in hard times, and he was damn swell at it too. Just in and out and nobody gets hurt. Hell, if he was in the "Auld Sod" they'd be singing songs of praise about him.

He swept the room with a motion of the gun's barrel and the customers dropped to the wood plank floor like trained monkeys. An elderly security guard stood frozen in a corner, eyes round and unblinking in fear. Beads of sweat freckled his upper lip. Frank sauntered to the cage, dropping the satchel on the counter. The small-town broad looked more like a barroom floozy than a bank teller. She had bleached Jean Harlow waves with dark roots and lips bright as a maraschino cherry in a Manhattan. She looked like she passed out her favors as easily as she counted out dollar bills.

From the floor he heard someone whisper, "It's him. It's the Blue-Eyed Bandit." Frank's lips curled in a cocky smirk. Damn but he loved that moniker. Some pimply cub reporter south of Chicago called him that and it had stuck. It fit him like a felt Fedora. Those eyes got him under more skirts than he could count. He wasn't like Charles Floyd, who'd hated the tag "Pretty Boy". Pretty'd been a swell dresser but he was a fool. Shit, the day the coppers pumped him with seventeen bullets all he could say was "I think I've been hit". The words of an idiot—or brilliant understatement. Frank suspected the former.

"Fill it up, Toots," he said, indicating the satchel with a tilt of his head. A flicker of recognition twinkled in her eyes, putting a come-on smile on her luscious lips. Any other day he'd have obliged, pounding her through the mattress 'til she was too weak to walk and he was spent. But today was all business, then on the road before the hot winds kicked up even worse. She'd have to settle for a tale to tell her grand-kids. After all, he was damn near legend.

The blondie was shoving the last of the bills into his bag when Frank heard the hammer-click behind him. He spun around, blasting the guard with five rounds before the guy could squeeze off a shot. The old man looked surprised as he folded to the floor, still holding the pistol with his withered fingers.

"Damn, fuck, shit" Frank muttered. He grabbed the loot, slammed his shoulder against the door, exited, and high-tailed it to his car. Tires screeched as he fish-tailed down the street and onto the open road.

The wind gusts pushed violently against the car. He gripped the steering wheel tightly to maintain control. His heart was pounding hard enough to punch a hole through his chest and come out dancing a jig on his belt buckle. Why? He asked. Why did the old geezer unholster his gun? Frank was a bank robber but he wasn't a killer; no punk who mowed down bystanders just to steal a headline. Frank had principles. It was the guard's doing, he told himself. It certainly wasn't *his* fault. Now things were changed forever. If the cops weren't chasing him the G-men would be. The last thing he wanted was Feds on his tail.

His guts were twisting hard enough to churn butter. His summer seersucker suit was glued to his sweaty skin. He rolled down the window, shoved his head out. A hot blast of air splattered his vomit onto the car's side. As he gasped, his mouth filled with dry Kansas dust that mixed with the sour bile caught in his throat.

It was getting more violent out there by the minute—and dark as a Mafia funeral.

* * * * * *

Maggie stood by the stove, stirring the simmering pot as she stared blankly out the window. As long as they had pigs there was food so they were better off than most. For now. One by one the pigs were dying, if not from hunger then from the dust that filled their lungs. The pigs were dying; their feed withered in the field; men were dying. Some men drowned in the sea of dust; some blew their brains out; some just gave up. The dust bowl turned men mad.

She sighed as she turned on the radio. Static filled the room. *"First Farmer's Bank...Ensign...Blue-Eyed Bandit...dead."*

At least there's some excitement out there, she thought with a cynical grimace. She spun the knob searching for band music. Gave up. Turned it off.

Pops came through the door, pulling off his protective mask, a huge cloud of dust in his wake. Turbulent and sinister. Maggie barely heard the pigs over the wind's roar, but their squeals always triggered something uneasy inside of her. Something she could never quite put her finger on. It gave her the heebie-jeebies and always reminded her of when Mom left. How old had Maggie been? Six? Seven? She remembered Mom's brisk goodbye. Pops had made little Maggie stay indoors as he followed Mom out. She sat abandoned, hands over her ears, silencing the frenzied squeals and restless snorts of those damned pigs.

When Pops came back in that morning he'd tried to explain that Mom was a city girl at heart. The loneliness out here tied down her spirit. He'd walked her up the road to catch the Dodge City bus. She'd be back, he had said, but from that day on his eyes were empty. She never came back.

Maggie snapped to the present, grabbed the broom and started sweeping for the thousandth futile time. The grit burrowed into everything—from their hair and bedding to the tub of lard in the pantry. It was enough to drive a girl crazy.

Pops mumbled something about the dirt being piled up to the window sills. And nonsense about how having a John Deere would make everything right.

Sure. And his pigs could fly.

* * * * * * *

Frank almost missed the barn's faint outline. He was near blinded by the thick, brown haze—and the image of a slain old man's sad, haunted stare as his eyes clouded over....

He hit the brakes, cut a sharp left, and aimed towards the welcoming shadow of the farmhouse.

Frank knocked and was pulled into the kitchen. The door slammed behind him. The heat was stifling. The room smelled of pig shit, stale sweat and despair. Layers of dirt coated everything, collecting deep and defiant in the corners. The gal who'd invited him in swept with the wrath of the damned, displacing the soil from one spot to another and back again. A man sat at the kitchen table studying gnarled hands with weary eyes. He had to be her father. She couldn't have been more than seventeen tops.

"Could I sleep the night in your barn, sir? It's wild and blind out there, not safe for...."

"No more doors, no more doors, no more sweeping, no more

doors." She chanted it like some mantra she'd repeated a thousand times, tossing the broom into the corner with a hollow clatter.

This little dame was a real looker. A deusy. The face of an angel with porcelain skin, hair the color of half-ripe strawberries, eyes green and wild as shamrocks.

Invited to eat with them and bed upstairs, Frank sat, sliding the bag of loot safely under his chair. His stomach thanked him loudly but he tasted nothing. Her cotton dress, paper thin from hundreds of washings, clung to her damp body, caressed her young breasts. His body responded and he was damn glad he was sitting down.

Later, Frank followed her to where he'd sleep. As she led him up the narrow stairwell his eyes followed the motion of her round, tight caboose. Damn but he wanted to dive into the sticky sweet magic between those gams. She opened a door and they entered the room. Frank tossed his satchel into a corner as she fluffed the bed pillow with a punch hard enough to cold-cock The Great John L. A cloud of dust flew from the pillow and she mumbled, "Enough dirt to drive one crazy."

Maggie walked over to where Frank stood, pressing her body against his as she looked into his intense blue eyes. Her voice was deep and smoky as her hot breath whispered in his ear:

"You can put your shoes under my bed any time."

Before you could say "John Dillinger" they'd disrobed, leaping into the bed, rusty bed springs creaking in protest. Sweaty bodies slid sensually against each other as she spread her legs and straddled him. Pressing him against her sweet damp folds she flexed soft pink muscles, milking his cock with them, pulling it into her. There was an urgency, a hunger, as she drove him into her forbidden depths.

Frank's day had started lousy, but now, in this humid little room on the outskirts of nowhere, everything was Jake.

She leaned forward, pulling a tattered head scarf from the nightstand drawer, not bothering to reclose it. She repositioned her hips atop him and said, "I wanna play." There was mischief in her eyes. She twirled the scarf into a blindfold and tied it securely around his head and over his eyes.

Life couldn't get better than this. This was payday. A bag of loot, a hot broad, and all the time in the world.

She ground her pelvic bone against him. Her moans said she was enjoying this as much as he was. Hell, maybe more. He thrust into her, over and over. It took all the self-control he could muster not to pop off right then and there. But he wanted to drown in her wild, animal sex forever.

Frank felt the weight of her against his chest as she stretched across him, heard her fingers shuffling through the nightstand drawer. His anticipation escalated with his breathing as he wondered what was next in this doll's bag of tricks. This was turning into the ride of his life. Impeccably Jake.

A flash of light and pain exploded behind Frank's eyes, bursting and spreading like fireworks on the fucking Fourth of July. His last conscious thought was the knowledge that he was wearing the same expression as the old bank guard.

Then darkness.

Then nothing at all.

Maggie kept his cock snugly inside of her as the ice pick penetrated into his brain, shoving and grinding it deeper into his ear canal like she was trying to crank up an old Model T. Deeper, deeper. She giggled as her body climaxed to the rhythm of his death throes. Then leapt from the bed.

Frank had given himself away the moment she'd opened the door and looked into amazing blue eyes. She knelt naked on the floor, her fingers running through the money from the Farmer's Bank heist. Her nostrils inhaled the pungent smell of government ink mixed with the oil of a thousand men's dirty hands. The sweet, filthy aroma of cold, hard cash.

She rose, putting the tattered dress over her head and shaking it into place with two snaps of her hip. "This fucking dust is enough to drive a girl crazy, crazy, crazy," she sang as she galloped down the stairs with child-like enthusiasm, black satchel in hand.

Maggie tossed the bag onto the kitchen table across from where Pops sat.

"Here's your John Deere, Pops," she said proudly.

With a slight turn of her torso, she stretched out her arm, pointing towards the stairwell.

The hot night wind blew mournfully, carrying the oinks and snorts of the pigs as they paced and choked in their pens. In that same split second something happened inside Maggie. The deep, gnawing unknown that had haunted her stopped. It coalesced into vivid, absolute clarity. In that moment, as the pigs screams rode the deadly wind, she knew. The mystery of her mother's departure was clear.

She knew.

She turned, locking eyes with Pops, still pointing awkwardly in the direction of the dead man beyond the top of the stairs. And as she spoke, Pops knew that she knew. Everything. She said:

"...and your pigs won't go hungry."

CRAWLSPACE

If there's one thing life's taught me, it's that life ain't fair. If it was I wouldn't have been sitting in the slammer waiting out a five year stint for robbery with nothing to read but the Bible and inspirational, self-help bullshit. One thing I learned from the Bible was that any one of those guys could have been my cell mate. That Cain guy murdered his brother. When Lot's wife got zapped and turned to salt, he did the nasty with his own daughter. I could go on and on, but you get the point. And I had to keep an eye on my backside, even while I was sleeping. The bastards put me away on nothing but one near-sighted eyewitness who couldn't have seen a damn thing. At trial, he pointed his finger at me like he'd actually seen me commit the crime. I stared him down, but he must've felt safe up there on the stand. Shit. Like I said, there was no evidence, no loot, no proof. Nothing but my extensive resume. What's fair about that? A long rap sheet always makes you the patsy. The cops and the courts take the easy way. They just haul you back in whenever somebody snatches an old lady's purse or poisons somebody's rat-mutt for yapping at midnight. The lawyers get paid, win or lose, so they don't give a shit. Especially those lazy, fucking public defenders. I feel bad for all the innocent dupes that get put away like I was—for nothing more than being in the wrong place at the wrong time. I'll bet there's plenty of 'em, too. Every thug and small time crook in prison swears he's innocent. Maybe, just maybe, a few of them are.

Some people might call me a loser. I never saw it that way.

The night before my ma's man left for 'Nam, she asked him to give her something to remember him by. She probably wanted an engagement ring... nine months later she got me instead. She never heard from him again, never knew if he was killed in action or just another run-off asshole. But what the hell, it got me into this world, didn't it?

It's funny how things play out.

I lived for Gloria's monthly visits. I could have set my watch on them, if I'd had one. That last time was a real corker. She sauntered in, her size-too-small dress clinging in all the right places. As she walked toward me, her hips churned like she was having sex. She sat down and picked up the phone so we could talk through the glass barrier. Her fingers slid up and down the receiver like she was playing with my poodle-dink. That wicked little wink told me she knew exactly what that was doing to me.

Damn, but she could tease.

"I miss you, baby," Gloria whispered. Her voice was like a smoke-filled barroom at midnight, fuzzy and filled with promises of drunken, dirty sex. We small-talked, but I was focused on those full, moist lips that could send me straight to heaven—and getting my walking papers. I wanted to screw her until she couldn't walk, just like in the old days.

Every visit Gloria'd tell me she was faithful—just waiting for the day I'd get out. I pretended I bought it, but I knew better. Gloria couldn't spend one night in an empty bed. It was how she was made, but that's what attracted me to her in the first place. She was eager and easy and I was willing and able. The down side was I knew she'd been out there straddling anything that was still breathing, but it don't matter that much. Once I got out she'd be all mine, just like before. I'd see to that. I might have to rough her up some before she got the idea, but she'd learn all over again. The occasional gut-punch works wonders for fidelity.

"I've decided to sell my house and find us better digs," she said, throwing me into panic mode.

"You can't do that."

Gloria looked startled. So I calmed my voice, and my heartbeat, before I continued.

"I get out in just over a month, Gloria." Her puzzled expression told me I needed to think fast. "I've spent five years thinking about the day I can walk up to that house with you greeting me at the door. It's what's kept me going." I hoped I was convincing. "Let me have that moment, baby. Then you can sell it."

I'd guessed she bought my line, blind to the wheels turning behind those baby blues.

I always underestimated broads, even the dumb ones.

They always meant trouble.

But every time they get me in the sack I forget every lesson I'd ever learned. I think with my dick. It's just my nature.

"Anything you say, baby," she said.

And like I said, she was easy.

She rose to leave and leaned forward until her face touched the glass. She opened her mouth as if to kiss me, then ran her tongue up the length of the barrier as if it were my cock. The paper thin dress fabric between her and the glass wiped up the dampness as she rose. Wet spittle outlined one perfect nipple. Gloria could tease a man to torment. She turned, tossing her bottle-blonde hair as she wiggled that tight ass of hers toward the exit. Every guard and inmate within sight of her had a hard-on, but mine ached beyond belief.

* * * * * * *

I stood outside the gates, the barbed wire fences and bad food behind me, fifty bucks in the pocket of my cheap prison-issue suit. I took a deep breath as I got onto the bus, inhaling the morning air and bus fumes. Simple things become precious when you don't have them. Air, good eats, simple freedom. I hadn't seen Gloria in a month and was heading straight for her house. She wasn't the only loose end I'd left when the cops snatched me from her porch, threw me in the squad car, and drove me straight to hell.

The bus pulled into the train station, brakes screeching like a two-year-old brat in a shopping cart. I got off and bought a ticket to that shit-hole town in Nebraska where Gloria would greet me with open arms and an open door. She'd stir up a home cooked meal like some frenzied June Cleaver on crack. She was my ideal and my whore all wrapped into one steamy package. It was gonna be a long ride, so I picked up a magazine to see how the world had changed, had kept spinning while I'd rotted in limbo. It wasn't fair. It was hard not to hold a grudge, so I held it tight against my heart. I nurtured it and let it grow like black mold on old cheese.

* * * * * * *

The train sped through the darkness, a cold steel snake, it's forlorn whistle cutting through the night like a sharp blade through soft flesh. The vibrations and jerks of wheel against track were hypnotic and sensual, taking me to those places every man goes who's been alone too long. I placed the magazine discreetly across my lap. I ached for Gloria's touch against my aching joint, erasing five years of fantasy stoked by imagination and memory—and my own hand. Hours later, I awoke to the moan of metal grinding against metal as the train pulled into the station. It was that eerie time of morning when darkness and day fight their battle of lights and shadows. The sun was hunkered down just below the horizon, a hungry cat ready to pounce. I never bought into that new day, new beginning crap. There was no such thing as a day that didn't get fucked up. God, if there was a god, got off on playing practical jokes. He laughed a lot. They say laughter is good for your health, so if he's up there he's gonna be there for a long, long time.

Anyway, it was six A.M. in the boondocks—the beginning of my first full day of freedom. I was feeling optimistic, all things considered.

I walked through the station carrying my small brown bag and my magazine. They hand you back your stuff when you leave prison. I had my toothbrush and the prison-issued clothes on my back. I tossed the magazine to the floor and walked through the door to the dusty street. It was a three mile walk to Gloria's place. In less than a mile the cheap shoes raised heel blisters and some stranger offered a lift as I limped along. He pulled his pickup to the shoulder. Lucky day. I stood at the end of Gloria's driveway in no time.

Damn, I was excited. Good shit comes to he who waits, right?

The closer I got to the door the more I got that feeling, like worms with sharp teeth gnawing at my stomach lining. It felt familiar and I didn't like it. The prison shrink called it panic attacks, but he'd never give me any happy pills to make it go away. On the outside some good "Irish" burning down my throat always helped some. As a kid, my mother called those knots my guilty conscience, but all she ever gave me for it was a hard swat up side the head. She'd say it was for one of the things I didn't get caught for. And there was plenty. There ain't nobody can see through a kid like his mother. I'd sneak into her whisky stash when I could and drink myself stupid. Self-medication is the stuff of the angels. I guess this time those nasty knots triggered when I saw the unfamiliar car parked out front. Things change in five years, maybe she'd bought a new one, but it didn't feel right. I was going to barge right in, catch her in the act—maybe beat up some poor jerk before I slapped her around, then forgave her. Stuff like that helped the gut knots go away. And Gloria got off on the drama. It made her hot—we fed off each other— the perfect match. Damn, I'd missed her. Ordinarily I don't like confrontation this early in the morning. It's something you gotta work up to, you know?

The door was locked.

So I knocked.

Really hard.

The guy that opened the door stood there in his bathrobe and looked at me like a tattered question mark, probably trying to place my face in his memory bank.

"Where's Gloria?" I bellowed, trying to push through him and past him.

He was strong for an old guy and was on me like a toad's tongue on a swamp fly before I knew what hit me. It was his fist. But it hurt his hand as much as it hurt my jaw, so I landed a good one below his rib cage while he paused to shake his aching hand. I lost my balance—landed on the hardwood floor with an undignified *thud*. That pissed me off, as you can imagine. He dove after me and I managed to trip him. He fell to the floor. I got myself upright before he could. Then I lost it. I kicked the holy shit out of him. He cowered in a fetal position and I didn't stop until he stopped moving. My stomach felt better already. He was still breathing as he looked up at me. He groaned something so muffled I could barely hear him.

The words finally registered.

"I bought this place a month ago," he'd said, then passed out.

That's when I went totally bug-shit.

I ran out the front door to the side of the house, kicked the lattice away and wiggled into the crawlspace, through the dust and spider webs and empty, rusting paint cans. I hate to say I was bordering on frantic, but that's what I was and there isn't a better word for it. I was so frantic that I dug in the dirt until my fingers bled. I was still digging long after I knew that the loot I'd hid was just as gone as Gloria. I'd never told Gloria I'd really done it. A guy has gotta cover his bases, right? But, even dumb as she was, she must have figured things out back when I told her not to sell the house. She'd probably gone through every square inch of the place until she found it. Female greed and pure determination won out. In my mind, I saw her on some tropical island, drinking something sweet and strong with a little pink umbrella in it, boasting a tan and laughing at me.

She was probably getting serviced by some gigolo with a moustache—named Julio or Enrique or something like that.

The heartless bitch.

I didn't like being laughed at.

Everything that happened, up to that and after that, was all

Gloria's fault. I've got nobody to blame but her.

My bloody fingers were still digging through dirt when the cops pulled up. I froze in my hiding place, stopped breathing, but eventually they spotted me. They pulled me out kicking and screaming and babbling, covered in spiders and sweat and dirt and my own piss, devoid of all dignity.

One more trip in the back of one more squad car. Hell, it was probably the same one. The scenario was getting too familiar. Like I said, there's no such thing as a perfect day. Seems the guy I'd roughed up came to long enough to dial 911 before he passed out again. Just my luck, right?

They grilled me for three days and nights. The dumbest question, the one that drove them nuts, was what the hell was I doing digging in the crawlspace? Damned if I would tell them. Then they'd know I was like every other con who'd swore he was innocent. It was the mantra of the incarcerated. I wouldn't give them the satisfaction of telling them the loot had been under their big, flat feet all the time. Of course, if they hadn't figured I was guilty from the get-go, I wouldn't have been put away for that robbery in the first place. The snakes were squirming around in my stomach again and I had no way to let off steam. My thought processes were starting to fog. Interrogations do that.

The morning of day four it hit the fan. The bastard I'd beaten up had died from his injuries. Things got fucking serious after that. The son of a bitch, I didn't hit him *that* hard.

Anyway, I'll spare you the details of the trial, the ankle chains, the long, boring ride to the penitentiary. For me it was just business as usual.

God sure as hell gave me the middle finger this time.

Thanks a lot, Gloria.

So, here I sit in a smaller cell in a bigger prison, reading the same old crap and sleeping with one eye open so I don't get it from behind, if you know what I mean. I've got lots of time to think. The rest of my life. Some things I still don't have quite right in my head. I wonder sometimes what I really miss the

most—losing the loot—losing my freedom—or losing Gloria.
Damn, I just don't know.
But I sure as hell miss her visits.

DEAD MAN'S DANCE

LAND'S END, CORNWALL 1649

High upon the cliff, overlooking the wild Cornish sea, the event unfolded in a mood as vacillating as the gray morning sky. The small crowd gathered like the overhead clouds, giggling, muttering, then silent, as shards of sunlight strangled in the thickening fog. The fingers of mist clung to the cliff-side as if they feared the churning sea below, then moved like tendrils around the half-obscured gnarl of twisted oak.

There was laughter, as if they'd gathered for a Sunday picnic, their voices muffled by the roar of waves crashing against solid rock. The sea spewed its vengeance upward toward the restless, hostile sky, its spray sifting downward to baptize the assemblage. They stood in a circle, and in the center of the circle stood he, tall and ominous, cloaked in black, stoic and still.

Waves of agitation rippled through the crowd as two men secured a rope on a high, sturdy branch of the old oak. One of them spoke to the other as he tightened the knot:

"Would'a be fittin' if the witch finder Matthew Hopkins were here for to find the rest of 'em heathens."

"Twenty shillings saved, for he'm be dead as salted mackerel, my dear Michael. An' besides, we don't be needing a furriner in our midst—bein' privy to business better handled by our own."

Michael fashioned a noose, then said, "We shoulda killed his wicked father before he spawned the divil by that disease-ridden wench—and better yet to have killed his father before him. But what of the others?"

"Eff the divil finally be dead they'm be getting back to the business o' healin' instead o' cursin' I should think."

"O' course, o' course," said Michael, but his voice held no conviction. His eyes glanced at the man in black as he lowered himself to the damp ground.

The wind gusted as the men reentered the crowd. The man was turned over to them, his hands tied behind his back. They held firmly to his arms, as if unsure the bindings could confine him, and pushed him beneath the oak. The man held his head high as he ascended the makeshift ladder, smiling at the gathering storm clouds. The wind caught the hem of his cloak, lifting it. It rose, billowing in a sensual dance around his tall, gaunt form. His face was chiseled, handsome; his eyes cold and gray as the slate cliffs, scanned the crowd.

To the back, a green eyed woman watched in silence. Her eyes met his, her secret lover, the man about to die. She looked down, expressionless as Michael slid the noose around his neck. The wind whipped her auburn hair across her face. A muscle twitched, distorting her features. She raised her head, muttered silently to the heavens, smiled. Her smile was radiant, the glaze in her eyes spoke of vile, obscene secrets.

The man in black tossed back his head and laughed.

Michael kicked the stool out from under him.

"The last generation of evil be gone." Someone screamed.

Then all was silent but for the moan of the wind and the steady creak, creak, creak of the oak's burdened branch.

Again the wind caught his cloak, whipped it around him as he spun madly, kicking and twitching, then fighting no more. As if hypnotized, they watched the dead man... dancing, dancing, dancing in a macabre circle.

"So be it," said Michael.

"We be doin' it like in other lands," bellowed the second man with authority, met with applause by the crowd. "A hangin' followed by a burnin' an' then that be the end of it."

One by one the people broke their trance, gathered twigs and piled them beneath the dead man's swaying form.

"This be for corrupting my sweet Mary" said a woman as she placed a branch on the heap.

"And for killing the wee newborn," whispered a young lad. "The poor little cheel."

"Let not a witch live," yelled Michael, stirring the crowd to frenzy.

As the other man knelt to light the funeral pyre there was a discernible depression in the atmosphere. The sky grew dark. The rain, which had been soft and teasing, pelleted down at an angry slant, extinguishing the flames. He relit it, fanned it with his large hands as the crowd chanted.

Again, the rain smothered it. The dense fog that blanketed the cliff-side was torn free by a violent gust of wind that howled eerily as the hounds of hell. People clung to each other to maintain their balance against the gale-force blast as the storm became a violent, unyielding flagh.

All eyes turned upward, following the groans and creaks from above their heads. The oak's branch cracked, then snapped, hurling its gnarled arm and the hanged man over the cliff.

Michael held his breath, watched as the body bounced against the granite rocks, then into the sea below. He watched as the waves swallowed the man, hungrily gulping at the floating black cloak until nothing remained but the fear in Michael's heart.

"The divil's work," he gasped as he stared down at the cold, wet grave.

"No, no, it be fittin' don't you scc?" The other man said in a strained, shrill voice. "'Tis an omen surely. He'm were put to cliff by the hand of God, like the bastard dog he were."

"'Tis true," someone muttered as the crowd huddled at cliff's edge.

"So be it."

"Amen."

The crowd dispersed, heading down-hill to the village of Petherick, back to the safety of their cottages. At the head of the procession the green eyed woman swayed as she danced and babbled a lunatic song. Her hand stroked her belly, just starting to swell with child. Sheets of cold rain lashed at her face, gusts of wind tore at her ragged shawl as she twirled about, singing, laughing—muttering words that held the key to dark and ancient knowledge.

THE ONE-EYED
BELLY DANCER

Her name wasn't Ahsin when she'd clawed her way out of the gutters and alleys of Nogales on the shit side of the border. The ten-year-old whore got streetwise fast and figured out men, and her version of life, early on. The nights were eternal, a diseased vision of the Day of the Dead, filled with skeletons and shadows, druggies, drunks, and starving, desperate mongrels. The other *poquito putas* wore out by fifteen. Hunger had been her only conscious sensation—she learned how to keep her stomach full. The trade-off was in black eyes, scars, bruises, humiliation. From her pimp. From customers. Sharp as a machete and twice as lethal, she wised up quickly.

"Pimps are for fools," she'd said to Sánchez, stepping over his fat body as he bled out on the dirty floor. She clenched the gun in her hand like a hot ticket to paradise. Getting across the border was easy. In Bisbee an old guy took her in, passed her off as his granddaughter. She got pretty clothes, an education, dance classes, anything she wanted. All she had to do was give him a blow job or thirty-second sex when he could get it up. The segue from used to user was as smooth as farting through silk pajamas.

When she'd taken what she could, she moved on and never looked back. Tucson was a far cry from Bisbee, with buildings taller than saguaros and opportunities for the taking. She wanted to dance. At the Eastern Oasis. But they had a dancer. A good one. The dancer crossed paths with Ahsin in the alley one night. An unfortunate accident, but the random corpse was common as *cholla* in this end of town. Ahsin walked into the job she wanted.

* * * * * * *

Ahsin spotted Raúl at his favorite back table, as expected. Handsome, rich, cool Raúl. A half-smile crossed her lips as painted fingers ran through her long, raven hair. Dark eyes and writhing hips mesmerized the audience. And Raúl. A small café in a Tucson strip mall, the Eastern Oasis was surrounded by run-down bodegas, bars, and fast food joints. But once inside one was enveloped by exotic spices, the reverberation of primitive instruments and drums—and Ahsin. Ahsin, Arabic for beauty. She was magic and mystery, conjuring lust and filling the cashbox with every twist of her hips. She was her best invention.

Raúl felt she danced for him alone. She felt the drum vibration between her legs as she danced, wove through the tables, stood where Raúl sat with his wife. Twenty years ago the wife might have been attractive, but to Ahsin she'd committed the one unforgivable sin—she was old. The woman wore an intricate diamond necklace, the sparkles dripping down her flat chest like leaves fluttering from a mesquite tree, while Ahsin flaunted the most glorious breasts money could buy. The diamonds shone in bright contrast to the weak reflections from Ahsin's sequined eye patch. For the four months of their affair, Ahsin puzzled why he lavished jewels on this woman. But that would change. She owned his body, but wanted his soul. And his bankroll.

She did a sensual shimmy, whispered *"Salaam alaikum"* as she leaned across their table. The wife ran her tongue along the margarita's salty crystals, scooped a mound of *baba ganoush* onto her pita, shoved it into her mouth. Ahsin winked at Raúl, knowing he'd meet her at midnight.

At home after the show, Ahsin showered and wrapped her naked body in a silken veil and answered the door. Raúl entered, unwrapped her, pressed his body against her flesh. Her nipples are dark as Hershey Kisses, he thought as he undressed. How perfectly it had started. The wife at home, this creature as his pleasure in the night until the next one came along. But she proved as addictive as heroin and twice as hard to kick. He needed his fix.

"Take off your eye patch," he said.

"Never. You're more evil than a thousand Bedouins and camel herders."

"How did it happen, *mi amor*?"

"We're all entitled to one flaw and one secret," she said. "¿Mysterioso, sí?"

She danced before him, removing the eye patch. His foreplay always focused on the empty eye socket. And the kinky tricks that drove him wild. What other woman could top that? It was her deal clincher and she played it. Then she pushed him inside her. Their rhythms synchronized. He climaxed. She slid from his perspiring flesh. Raúl was mediocre between the sheets, but his obsession and his money were definite turn-on's.

"We're perfect for each other," she said, twirling his chest hair with her finger, "but we can't keep on like this. It's killing me."

He sighed. "Me too." What could he do? He wanted her 24/7 and didn't know how far he was willing to go, how much he wanted to sacrifice. She was a sex machine, uninhibited, every man's lurid fantasy. But the wife had something important too. He held Ahsin close. "You know I love you."

"Words are no longer enough," she said, the luxuries his money could buy swimming in her head. She wanted it all, not just bits and pieces tossed her way like promises on the wind. She deserved the whole enchilada. She toyed with his penis as it hardened under her touch, bewitching him into compliance. Lesson number one: Touch a man's dick and his brain ceases to function. "Leave her or we're done." Her words slapped him limp.

His silence filled the room. The status quo was dandy, but

could he bear losing her? Finally he spoke: "I'll leave her. Friday night it'll be over."

"And we'll have just begun."

They made love again. She'd negotiated perfectly.

"I never thought I'd want to live without her money," he said. "But we'll have each other and we'll do fine."

His words spun her into a dark abyss. Fine? The bitch bought her own jewels? Bought HIM? Now it made sense. Suddenly Raúl was less handsome. She noticed the track of pock marks above his suave moustache, smelled the faint rancid aroma of his sweat, heard the annoying hint of weakness in his voice. Raúl wasn't as debonair as he'd been just five minutes ago. And his fucking pockets were empty.

"Until Friday," she whispered.

* * * * * * *

The Oasis was packed with the usual Friday night crowd. Shish-kebab flamed and sizzled, glasses clinked, conversation in Arabic, Spanish and English bounced off the deep ochre walls. As Ahsin walked dramatically through the curtain, drums and hearts pounded. The room fell silent as she raised her arms above her head, hands in delicate pose. She stood Venus de Milo still, then hips quivered, ground, to the escalating music, her midriff rolling to the beat. Lost in the music, her exquisite form floated, creating its magic. She danced as never before, with a wantonness and splendor worthy of the gods, the wealthiest of Sultans. And she knew it.

That slick bastard Raúl smiled, tossed her a wink. The wife was bejeweled in the splendor of a sheik's palace, as though Raúl had emptied the contents of a safe deposit box onto her bony chest, withered arms, drooping earlobes. Centered on her wrinkled neck sat one, perfectly colored, solitary emerald—the size of a quail's egg.

Ahsin danced to their table. The crowd ceased breathing as she arched her spine, bent backwards, locked eyes with the wife. Her hand stroked the woman's face in slow, sensual whispers, her tongue slid up her neck letting the bitch feel her hot breath. Slowly Ahsin rose, thrust a hip forward, danced away. The crowd exhaled a communal sigh as she exited through the curtain, propelled by thunderous applause.

Ten minutes later Ahsin reappeared in haughty pose, rotated her shoulders as she stepped forward.

"It's missing. My emerald is gone."

Pandemonium filled the room. The inconsiderate bitch had blown her entrance, drawing attention to herself. The room belonged to HER, to Ahsin. The crazy woman ranted like she'd lost the only precious stone she owned. It was downhill from there. Customers were searched. It hit rock bottom when they had the nerve to search Ahsin. They found nothing. Raúl and spouse pushed through the crowd to the exit amid apologies from a stunned management. Raúl whispered "Give me one extra hour," as he passed Ahsin. She nodded and smiled.

* * * * * * *

In the car, Raúl comforted his wife. When they arrived home it was all clear. He should have thought of it sooner. The perfect solution. And it was far easier than he thought. The headline would read something like this: Drunken Heiress Falls to Death from Balcony. When he looked down she was nothing but a rumpled splat on a large stone in the cactus garden below. The moon's reflection shimmered on the heated pool, the city lights laughed in the distance.

He called 911. Then he called Ahsin to tell her he'd be late—that as soon as the insurance paid off they'd have it ALL...there was no answer.

There was no answer at all.

* * * * * * *

Ahsin crossed the border at Nogales and checked into a

crumbling adobe motel. She tossed her purse onto the bed, sat in a cracked plastic lawn chair in the corner. A low voltage bulb was the room's only light. She was a barely discernible shadow as she slipped the eye patch over her head and dropped it onto the table. It had served her well. Her right hand raised, she dug deep into the empty eye socket. Pay dirt. Slowly her fingers slid out of the hole, releasing the emerald from its hiding place. She walked back to the bed, removed the glass eye from her purse, popped it into the empty socket. In her head, Middle Eastern music was replaced by Mariachi as she danced joyously, floated across the room clutching the precious stone in her fisted hand. Drop, kick, thrust. Shimmy, shimmy turn.

"This will go a long way south of the border". She sang, never knowing her single stone could have been a thousand.

* * * * * * *

By early morning light, Ahsin threw on a peasant blouse, stepped into worn cotton capris, shoved the emerald into her pocket. She threw her purse over her shoulder as she stepped into her sandals and out the door. Daylight was dusty, harsh, the town nothing but a faint memory best forgotten. Heading towards the jeweler her feet drew her like a siren's song to the familiar alley that had been her home.

Little whores with empty eyes were strewn in the shadows like yesterday's garbage. Ahsin held her head high, knowing she'd always been better than them, always deserved more. She was Ahsin. Unnoticed, the emerald slipped through a hole in her worn pocket, landed in the dirt and grime along her path as she strutted by.

A young girl, boney and gaunt, saw something shining through the dust at her feet, bent down, picked it up.

"Joya esplendido," she gasped, a faint glimmer of life returning to her weary eyes. Lying in her palm, sparkling with promise, was her ticket out of town.

IRREFUTABLE EVIDENCE

Marnie Jensen stood in front of the full length mirror in her bedroom and slowly undressed, shedding the costume she wore to the office. It was her uniform of respectability in the business world. She unbuttoned her proper wool suit jacket and tossed it onto the bed. The work day was behind her and it was time to relax, to be herself again. She pulled off the soft blue sweater that matched her eyes, then kicked off her shoes and wiggled her skirt onto the floor. Unsnapping her lacy bra, she pivoted in a circle, then stepped out of the thong that hugged her Brazilian waxed mound, exposing the temporary vagi-tattoo; a tiny purple tulip, its petals pointing to her soft blonde landing strip.

She stood as still as a marble statue in a museum, assessing her naked reflection, at the way the lights and shadows from the late afternoon sun and the autumn leaves from the neighbor's towering oak played across her body like a thousand fingers softly caressing her skin. Removing the barrette that held her ash blonde hair, she ran her fingers through its strands as it cascaded to her shoulders. With a toss of her head she blew a kiss at her reflection, then turned and walked across the room.

* * * * * * *

Jared was in his favorite place, his tree house up in the old oak tree, thumbing through the old issue of *Playboy* he'd found under his father's mattress. It was easy to see why his father had saved the old thing, as well as why he kept it secreted from his mother. And his father couldn't say a word if he ever discovered it missing from its hiding place. Now Jared could keep it hidden up here in his tree, in the beaten up foot locker he kept in the corner. It was the old May 1968 issue with Playmate of the Year, Angela Dorian, on the cover. Pages 134 through 139 were well-worn, the pages Jared looked at over and over. Angela sitting on the hood of her pink car. Angela lying in the grass, her generous breasts exposed to the sun. Angela pouting at the camera. Those girls his mother kept trying to fix him up with from Temple Emanu-El couldn't compare to that hot Sicilian in *Playboy*.

But his next door neighbor, Marnie, came damn close.

She was in her late twenties and single. And her bedroom, with its wrought iron balcony and sliding glass door, faced the old oak tree. She never bothered to close the drapes, most likely because the room didn't face the street. But it did face the branches of her neighbor's oak, providing quite the peep show to the adolescent next door.

Especially when she had male company, which was frequently.

Jared's father had built the tree house for him for his fifth birthday and it was the best damn present he'd ever received. It was better than those stupid action figures or model car kits that the other kids would bring to his birthday parties—or even the books his parents, Marty and Sarah, had deemed age appropriate for their little genius. Everything they gave him was geared to developing his intellect at an early age, even the music. They'd read somewhere that exposing young children to Bach exercised parts of their brain that would enhance their SAT scores later in life. Jared had every note of the Brandenburg Concertos etched in his brain before he was out of diapers. His mother had probably started playing it for him when he was still in the womb. One can't start too early. And Jared was their prize. Surely he was the world's next Albert Einstein and in their parental pride they knew he was the most brilliant child ever born. They treated him accordingly, pushing him, praising him, smothering him to distraction.

But all Jared wanted was to be left alone.

His tree house was his refuge.

His secret life.

His escape from people. He didn't care much for what he referred to as the common herd, and preferred solitude over socializing. He didn't like the kids in school and they didn't like him much either. And most adults bored him as well. Especially teachers who tended to have knowledge merely one chapter ahead of the class. Jared never saw the point in small talk, something his mother considered a necessary social skill. And he saw no point in trying to fit in with a group of kids who couldn't think any deeper than the latest celebrity gossip or reality show or dreaming of the day they'd get their learner's permits. Their teasing didn't touch him. He was confident that he'd have the last laugh. Right now he might be the geeky outsider, but while they were surely doomed to a life of pumping gas or making hamburgers, married to some painted Lady GaGa wannabe, he'd be the next Bill Gates. He'd live in a mansion, count his money, and have a hot chick on his arm. Or, better yet, several. All the girls back in school who never gave him a second glance would wish they had done so when they had the opportunity.

He still remembered his fourth birthday party. They'd invited the usual relatives and neighborhood kids, as well as old man Friedman from across the street. He hadn't liked Friedman from day one. And Friedman didn't like him. The old man was nosy, opinionated and coarse. And his breath always reeked of garlic and sickeningly sweet Manischewitz wine. Jared had opened his stupid presents, ignored his guests and settled quietly and comfortably into a corner, far from the laughter and chattering.

"Jared, sweetie," his mother had said, "thank everyone for your presents." Sarah tugged at her son's arm and steered him across the room. He mumbled his thanks, eyes to the floor. And old man Friedman snorted an audible "Hrrrumph."

Jared heard Marty whisper to Sarah, "It's only a phase, I'm sure he'll outgrow it."

Sarah just sighed her well-practiced martyrs sigh, tilting her head towards her son, to indicate what she saw as a problem.

But Jared saw no problem at all.

He closed his *Playboy* and returned it to the footlocker, rusted hinges creaking as he lifted the lid. He removed his copy of Schrodinger's Cat, on the quantum theory of superposition. Well, Jared had a few theories of his own on that subject. He lifted out *The Complete Works of Shakespeare* and placed it on top of the Schrodinger book on the floor. (His parents wanted his knowledge to be well-rounded.) Then he lifted out the false bottom of the footlocker and returned the *Playboy* to its hiding place atop his other hidden treasures, covered it with the false bottom, put back the books and slammed the lid shut. He heard a sound, like metal sliding along well oiled metal, and looked out the small tree house window. Towards the neighbors. Marnie stood there in all her glorious nakedness, sliding open the glass door that led from her bedroom to the small balcony, letting the evening breeze kiss every flawless inch of her. Damn, but he loved when she came home from work. And the weekends. He could watch her forever. She was like looking at a Renoir masterpiece, like Amelie Dieterie in a White Hat, its palette of soft pastels a myriad of subtle peach tones and muted creams and delicate whites. The girls he met at schul jangled the senses like the bold, harsh colors in an abstract by Alfred Gockel. Caustic. Like his mother.

"Jared, Jared, baby, it's time for dinner." Sarah called from the back door. "Jaaaa-red." Fifteen years in California hadn't erased a note or a nuance. No matter how hard she tried to get rid of it, the Long (pronounced Lon-G, with a hard G) Island twang that remained in her voice was unmistakable. After a couple glasses of wine it returned full force, or when relatives would drop in from back east for a visit at which time she'd reabsorb the accent like a sponge. When they'd leave she'd start practicing all over again, to no avail. It annoyed him like an irritating scab that refused to heal. His mother's voice was like brittle fingernails rubbing against sandpaper, harsh and abrasive and an assault upon the senses.

He leapt onto the ladder and swiftly descended down the rungs that were nailed helter-skelter along the trunk of the tree. His tree. The sooner he got back into the house, the sooner she'd stop yelling out for him and the sooner he could return to his refuge.

They sat at the dinner table, his mother giving him the third degree while his father sat there in his usual passive silence, slowly pushing his food around his plate with his fork, head down.

"Did you finish your homework?"

"At lunch."

"How did you do on the math test?"

"A-plus."

"And science?"

"A-plus."

His father took another mouthful of brisket and exhaled a soft sigh.

"Are you preparing well for Bar Mitzvah? Have you been going over your haftorah? It's less than two weeks away, Jared," she said.

"Yes, and have you got every pot and pan and dish rearranged so that when Aunt Sophie comes from Buffalo she'll think you're keeping a kosher kitchen?" There was a note of sarcasm in Jared's voice.

"Tsk, tsk, tsk," said his father. "You must treat your mother respectfully."

"Sophie'd have an aneurism if she knew she was eating unclean," Jared said. Not that he really gave a shit, but it was fun throwing his mother's inconsistencies in her face from time to time. The fact that she had a public persona that didn't jive with the mother behind the four walls of their home didn't go unnoticed. Not only did he see it as an inconsistency, but a downright fraud. It amazed him that she was unable to see it herself.

Ignoring them both, Sarah continued her litany. "And the day after Bar-Mitzvah we're holding a banquet that will impress everyone. You really need to brush up on your social skills,

Jared. All the mishpachas will be there. And pretty girls, too."

"Mishpachas, mother? *Sarah.* They're called relatives. With you it's harder than trying to teach the English language to one of those wetbacks on Van Nuys Boulevard. You're not in New York anymore. This is California and it's the twenty-first century."

"Now, now," said his father.

"You sound more like a matchmaker from the old country than a mother." He continued, "What do you want from me? I get perfect grades, I've already been pushed ahead two years, and you want I should be a social butterfly on top of it? You want I should be a football star, too? Give me a break, okay?" He relished in mocking her east coast phraseology, even if it flew over her head faster than a jet plane full of tourists heading for Hawaii.

"I'm just saying—there'll be presents for you. And money, lots of it. You'll have a good nest egg towards your college education. *Oif drei zakhen shtait di velt: oif gelt, oif gelt, oif gelt.*"

That was one of his mother's favorite quotes: the world stands on three things: money, money, money.

"If I were a rich man, ladedadedadeda." Jared taunted.

She chose to ignore him. "And there will be important guests, Jared. People that are important to us socially. Just show a little appreciation now and then, that's all your poor mother asks." She sighed her best long-suffering sigh.

"I ask you, is this my rite of passage or your social opportunity?"

His father looked up and muttered under his breath, "I wonder if we should be celebrating the day you become a man or if we should be sitting shiva for you."

Jared heard the engine of Marnie's little Miata start up, then slowly back out of her driveway.

"Oy," said his mother. "That Marnie shiksa is shameful. So many men come and go from that house that I wonder if it isn't a *heizel.*"

He detected a slight smile at the corner of his father's mouth, but all that passed through his lips was another sigh.

His parents were good at sighing.

"Whorehouse, mother," Jared corrected. In California it's called a whorehouse, not a heizel. If we were in London you could call it a knocking shop, but we're in California."

"So where did you learn such language?" She asked. "You should have your mouth washed out with soap."

Jared wolfed down a few more quick bites of his dinner and pushed back his chair.

"Yes, mother. Whatever you say."

"Don't you want some kugel, sweetie? Or more vegetables? It's important you eat your vegetables...." His mother's voice droned on and on from a distance as he headed back to the welcome silence of his tree house.

* * * * * * *

It was twilight, the time when darkness began winning it's nightly battle over the last glimmer of daylight. Jared crawled onto the oak branch like an iguana, inching cautiously along the rough bark. He looked down and saw old man Friedman on the sidewalk across the way. He was walking his ugly little, what did he call it? A peek-a-poo, or a cock-a-billybob or some such title, meant to hide the fact it was nothing but a mutt. The dog wasn't a breed at all, merely the result of some accidental inbreeding due to a hole in somebody's back fence. Jared froze, lest he be noticed, and waited until the old man was out of sight before he continued his journey. Marnie was gone, the sliding door that led into her bedroom open and inviting.

The nearer he came to his destination the thinner the branch became. He knew it wouldn't be long until he weighed too much to chance it. But for now... well. Jared swung like a pimple-faced Tarzan at the brink of puberty toward the wrought iron railing and nearly missed. His heart pounded as his hands grasped at the rail, held it in a tenuous grasp that left him dangling somewhere between a bad fall and his target. Slowly, he pulled himself up and across the balcony and into Marnie's bedroom, his heart pounding through his chest and up into his head and drumbeating at his temples. He threw himself onto her bed and lay there frozen until the pounding stopped and his breathing returned to some semblance of normalcy. It had been a close call this time. First, almost being spotted by Friedman, and second, nearly falling to his death. Or at the very least a broken bone or two.

Marnie's bed smelled like a field of wild flowers and Jared buried his face in her pillow, inhaling the essence of his boyish fantasy. Marnie. Blonde and beautiful and sexy. She was his dream girl, the image he called up every time he...

He rose from the bed and walked over to the bureau, opening the narrow top drawer that held her treasure trove of goodies. A small bundle of fragrant lavender sachet, encased in a delicate netting and tied with a tiny satin ribbon. Lace undies in every shade of pastel as well as deep blood red, push-up bras, scanty little thongs that were hardly there at all. He ran his fingers across them and closed his eyes. He inhaled the faint scent of her perfume. He fantasized. Then he closed the drawer and walked toward her master bath at the far end of the bedroom. He walked through its door and looked around, until he spotted the clothes hamper against the wall. He rummaged through the dirty clothes like a frantic bargain hunter at a swap meet until he found his prize. He pulled out the thong he'd seen her take off earlier, ran it past his nostrils, inhaled, then shoved it into his pants pocket.

From outside he heard the soft purr of her Miata as it rolled up the drive. She was back early. His heart pounded as he ran to the balcony, leapt onto the oak branch and scurried across to safety, like a rat abandoning a sinking ship. He was already back in his tree house by the time he heard her car door slam.

He removed her thong from his pocket, opened the foot locker, removed the false bottom and placed it among his treasures, which included other items from her lingerie drawer, collected during other night safaris to his neighbor's house. Jared wiped the perspiration from his brow and took a deep breath. For a non-athletic kid he got plenty of exercise during his little soirees. And tonight had been downright aerobic.

As he slammed down the lid, Jared heard another car pull up her drive and looked over. Marnie greeted the driver with a hug as he exited his car and they walked arm in arm up the pathway that led to her front door. She'd picked one up in record time tonight. The door slammed behind them as they entered her house. Jason positioned himself at the tree house window and looked across to her balcony.

It was getting dark, but when the bedroom light switched on the two of them stood there as if on the stage of some dirty Tijuana bar. The man was tall and muscular and seedy looking, like a character in a bad 1940s noir movie, right down to his thin, pencil moustache and swarthy complexion. Jared couldn't help but wonder at her taste in bed partners. She didn't seem to be choosy, but she certainly could have been. They marched in and out of her bedroom and in and out of her life like a line of ants seeking out sweet crumbs. And, oh how sweet she was— and more than willing to share her treats with an assortment of strangers. Sometimes the guys looked like college students, wearing their varsity letters, impatience and anticipation on their young faces. Some looked like the leftovers at the bars when it was closing time. And at other times they were old enough to be her father. But he rarely, if ever, saw one return for a repeat performance. It was obvious to him that she preferred the anonymity of one night stands. The men in her life serviced her, nothing more. She had sex with them and dismissed them without as much as a second glance. They were nameless and disposable and never had the opportunity to complicate her world.

Jared watched as tonight's man undressed her in record time.

And waited, wishing it was himself holding her naked body against his.

Swarthy pulled his black turtleneck over his head, then

reached in his pocket, removing a small, shiny packet. He stepped out of his slacks, ripped open the packet with his teeth, and handed the condom to Marnie. She knelt before him and rolled it into place. Then he grabbed her under the arms, pulled her up like she was nothing more than a rag doll and threw her onto the bed. She was laughing as he went at her like a bull in heat. Jared could hear a soft squeal escape her lips and vibrate through the tree branches, across the darkness of the night and into his ears.

He closed his eyes and listened.

When Jared opened his eyes she and Swarthy were standing again, holding their bodies against each other, Marnie whispering something softly into his ear. The man laughed as his hands explored the length of her body, pausing at her breasts. And then his hands were around her neck. Her eyes bulged in surprise as he tightened his grip on her throat, smiling. He fed on her fear as she tried to fight him, but she was no match. As the pressure on her neck increased, Smarmy stared intently into her eyes and watched as the last flicker of life drained from them.

Jared heard a soft popping noise as the bone in her neck broke beneath his grip.

Everything played out in slow motion before Jared's eyes and it seemed like forever before her limp body fell to the floor.

"Holy shit!" Jared muttered under his breath as he scrambled down the ladder. Before he'd even reached the back door he heard a car engine start up, and the sound of its motor diminishing in the distance as it drove down the street and far into the night, unseen.

* * * * * * *

The next day was Saturday. Jared sat at the kitchen table in silence. It was nearly noon and he was afraid to go to the tree house. Just the thought of what he'd seen the night before, and the image of Marnie as she lay dead on her bedroom floor, terrified him. So he just sat there, thumbing through a book, pretending he was studying as thoughts spun like rogue planets in his head. Could he have helped her? Unlikely. It all happened so fast. And someone would have known he was watching. He didn't want to explain that scenario. How long would she lie there, unnoticed? Did he dare tell anyone what he had seen? He knew he couldn't say a word without revealing a part of himself he'd rather not share with anyone. Especially his parents. Not that he was ashamed of his secret pastime, he doubted there was a kid out there who would've turned down the opportunity to watch Marnie. That was certainly one commonality he shared with other boys his age. Curiosity. He just figured it wasn't anyone's business but his own. So he chose to remain silent. It was the only logical thing to do.

Jared rose to the sound of loud banging on Marnie's door and went to the window. More banging at the door. The woman, tall and pale and not as pretty as his neighbor, was yelling, "Marnie! Marnie!" He observed her as she made her way along the walkway, overturning decorative stones until she found the right one. She lifted it, turned it upside down, and opened the secret compartment. She removed the spare house key, threw the stone back into the flower bed, and headed back to the front door, high heels clicking loudly on the cement.

About three minutes later Jared heard the screams.

* * * * * *

By mid-afternoon the light from several squad cars spun madly in front of Marnie's and a crowd of neighbor's was gathering as Jared watched from the safety of his living room. As they stood on the front lawn, old man Friedman was talking to one of the officer's. His arms were flapping around like a fish out of water, his eyes bulging as he spoke. Every once in awhile he'd point a finger in the direction of Jared's house and the cop would look in Jared's direction and nod. Jared backed away from the curtain as his parents entered the room.

"What is going on?" asked Sarah.

"I don't know," said Jared. "There's cop cars all over the place."

And next thing he knew his parents had dragged him out the front door as they joined the crowd of neighbor's amassing on the sidewalk. Gossip and rumors spread among them faster than flies on dog shit as they exchanged the bits and pieces they had gathered.

"Stand back," a cop was saying, "Clear out of the way so we can do our job."

Friedman held his little mutt in his arms. He leaned in close to them and filled them in on what he'd been able to gather, proud to be the one who could answer some of his neighbor's questions. Jared got a whiff of his unmistakable garlic breath and took a step backwards. As best they could gather, he said, Marnie was supposed to meet her sister for brunch and never showed up. And she didn't answer her cell phone or her land line. Heaven knows how long before she'd have been discovered if her sister hadn't come by looking for her. There were lots of theories and questions about what had happened, but there was one thing they all knew for sure. Their neighbor was dead.

"I knew she'd come to no good end," said Sarah. "That ilk always does."

"Sarah, Sarah," said her husband Marty. "You know it's not right to speak ill of the dead."

"I'm just saying...." Her voice drifted off as someone else caught her attention.

"She was a successful businesswoman, is what I heard," said another neighbor. "Insurance or something like that. Things like this just don't happen here."

"What's the world coming to when we aren't even safe in our own neighborhoods?" asked Sarah.

The crime scene investigators were still photographing the scene and dusting for prints as it neared dusk. As night fell, Marnie was wheeled down the walkway, zipped securely into a body bag, removed from the premises and into the waiting van, leaving all the mystery and unanswered questions behind her. There was no doubt that she met with foul play. The bruises on her neck and the subconjunctival hemorrhaging in her eyes made it obvious to police at the crime scene that she'd been strangled. But she was on her way to the morgue, and an ugly autopsy. They'd be slicing and dicing her as well as prodding her bodily orifices in search of DNA and any other evidence that might help lead them to her killer.

The neighborhood crowd slowly dissipated, as one by one they returned to their homes, homes that no longer felt safe, locking and dead bolting their doors behind them.

The police work had barely begun.

Two days later the police were canvassing the entire block, knocking on doors and asking questions. Had anybody seen anything unusual? Had anybody seen someone hanging around the neighborhood who was unfamiliar? Where were you on the night of the murder?

When Jared came home from school, his parents were sitting in the living room with two officers. Nobody ever sat in that room. It was the room in which Sarah kept plastic covers on all the furniture, exactly as it had been delivered from the showroom floor. Even the lamp shades still wore their plastic wrappings. Another senseless tradition passed down from mother to daughter. Some things just were and there was no point in asking why. And now there were cops sitting on the couch that he'd never been allowed to sit on?

"Jared," said his mother, motioning him to a chair. "Come sit down, sweetie. These gentlemen have a few questions."

"We've been questioning all the neighbors," said cop number one. He continued, asking all the same questions he'd been asking all day. No, Jared hadn't seen any strangers, no he saw nothing out of the ordinary, yes, he was just sitting at home doing his studying, as always.

Then cop number two directed his next comment to Marty, who appeared to be the most cooperative of the group. "We've been asking all the neighbor's to help us, sir. We're collecting

DNA swabs and fingerprints from everyone who will provide them voluntarily. You see, the sooner we can eliminate people, the easier it will be for us to zero in on the perp. Would any of you have a problem with that?"

Jared held his breath. Could he have left prints in Marnie's bedroom? What if they'd found prints there, then what? How could he explain that? He didn't want anyone to find out he'd been sneaking around when Marnie was gone. It would be embarrassing, to say the least. An uneasy knot filled his gut with apprehension. Sarah protested at what she considered not only an invasion of their privacy, but also a veiled accusation that they would somehow be capable of such a horrendous deed.

But, after reassuring them that they were not suspects and that it was nothing more than an investigative process, the cops got their swabs and their prints and were on their way to the next house.

Two days later the same two cops knocked on the door. Sarah opened the door and they handed her their search warrant. They went through every room of the house, opening and closing drawers and closets, snooping in all their rooms.

"Such a mess," she said. "What is this? A piece of paper and you can come in and turn my home upside down? Are we in Nazi Germany? Are you the damn Gestapo? This is an outrage, an assault on humanity." And on and on she droned.

"Sorry, ma'am," said cop number one, offering no explanation. "We'll be finished up shortly," and the two cops headed out the back door. Jared watched from the kitchen window as they both climbed up into the tree house. When they left, one of them was carrying a large evidence bag.

Jared was feeling sick to his stomach.

* * * * * * *

The next time the cops showed up at their door, it was with an arrest warrant in their hands. They pushed their way through the doorway, despite Sarah's protests.

"Is your son here?" asked cop number two, and it went downhill from there. Sarah was yelling and screaming and protesting and Marty was hush-hushing her in an attempt to calm her down.

"Jared! Jaaaa-red!" she yelled.

Jared finally peered around the corner into the hallway where they all stood.

"I don't understand, I don't understand," she was crying.

"Several items of your neighbor's lingerie were found out back in the tree house," said cop number one.

"You're accusing my son of being a ganef? A thief of that whore's undergarments?"

"And his DNA was all over them."

"Oy, my God, Jared! You've been up in the tree house playing with your schmeckle?"

Marty looked at his wife, sympathy filling his eyes. She just wasn't getting where this was going.

"You both have the right to be present at headquarters when we question your son," said cop number one as cop number two eyed Jared, who stood there frozen.

"Gestapo!" Sarah screamed. "You arrest a young man for touching his schmeckle?"

"On several occasions, your neighbor, Mr. Friedman, observed your son climbing across the oak branch and into the bedroom of your neighbor. And Jared's fingerprints were all over Marnie Jensen's bedroom," said cop number two. "What happened, Jared? Did she come home and catch you there? Is that why you murdered her?"

"Impossible," Sarah screamed. "This is impossible. My son would never do such a thing. He's a genius. He's special. He'd never.... Marty," she said, turning to her husband, "it's a week to Bar Mitzvah. What are we going to do?"

The first cop handcuffed Jared and lead him to the front door and out to the waiting squad car. His parents followed behind them, arguing all the way.

"Bar Mitzvah is the least of our worries," Marty said to his wife. "I think our biggest problem is whether he's going to be charged as a juvenile or as an adult."

THE WATERCOLOR
WITNESS

Tucson in August scorched like a cup of McDonald's java. Heat rose from the pavement like an apparition from hell, shimmered like a thousand rattlesnakes rising from hibernation. On the Fourth Avenue sidewalk Doobie stood, portable easel before him, brush in hand. Perspiration burned his eyes. The Saturday panhandlers and crazies encroached on his space, begged or ranted or told him about Jesus. Passersby paused to watch him paint—buildings, cars, buses, trolleys—they assumed he was another starving artist. Some offered an insulting ten or twenty. "Not for sale," "Fuck off," he'd say, dismissing them with a wave of his hand. His responses fell short of polite. Doobie wasn't starving. He wasn't even hungry. His watercolors topped the thousand dollar mark and his one-man shows sold out. He loved to paint. He loved his cats. He loved his pot and Japanese sake. He viewed people with contempt. Yoriko was the only exception. Doobie was pushing seventy. Yoriko was barely legal with the body of a twelve year old. She was his lover and his latest muse.

The heat was causing the paint to dry before it hit the paper. He rose, frustrated, focused his digital camera, clicked off ten shots before packing it in. One good shot of the trolley, a car passing on the left, ass end of a bus heading south. That one had possibilities. Painting outdoors was crazy in this heat and impossible during monsoon season, so he shot photos and painted in the air conditioned comfort of his studio. Today had become one of those days. A bit of a cheat by his standards but it got the job done.

Doobie shoved his supplies into the back seat then settled behind the wheel. Traffic pulled over to the side as a cop car flew past, blasting its shrill siren. He waited impatiently. Tucson was turning from calm to chaos—too much traffic, noise, crime— too many people. Not as crowded as the San Francisco he'd left behind but not good either. He'd always miss the early days in SF. He'd been part of the beatnik heyday—drugs, jazz, group sex, literature and art—a feast for the senses. It was inspirationally cool, man. Before the hippies descended on the Haight. They were the pretenders. The beats had been the real thing.

* * * * * * *

Doobie and Yoriko sat in silence, Sunday sunlight streamed across the table as they sipped herbal tea and shared an herbal joint as she read the morning paper. He never read the paper, had no interest in the outside world. Painting and Yoriko were enough to fill his universe.

She broke the silence.

"Three drive-bys on the south side, Doobie. Another body in the desert. A jewelry store robbed on Fourth. A van full of illegals crashed north of Tubac."

"Forget that crap," he said, pulling her from her chair and into the bedroom. That always got his artistic juices flowing. The vase of peacock feathers on the night stand were more than decorative and his imagination on the mattress was matched only by his creativity with brush and paint. That, not to mention his money and Sabino Canyon address, made him damn attractive to a young nubile chick.

Life was good.

* * * * * * *

Big Jim Bullock holstered his gun, put on his uniform and

badge, as Paco sat in an easy chair reading the Thursday paper. Last year Jim had answered a call to a downtown gay bar. It was two in the morning when he'd pulled up. Five men were kicking the shit out of a kid. He was bloody as a slaughterhouse. Your typical gay bashing. Unmacho didn't play well in Latino circles. Paco lay on the pavement, barely conscious. A wounded bird. A little sparrow. Big Jim's heart damn near broke. The paramedics patched up Paco on the way to St. Mary's. Big Jim was there when he was released. He took him home. Paco was his project, needy and grateful, passive and passionate. He needed to be pampered and protected. And Big Jim Bullock was a cop. Protecting was his job.

"Oooh, Chim," Paco squealed, "Look, Doobie has a new show. Artist reception Saturday." Paco, and most of Tucson, devoured this section of the Thursday paper. It listed shows, restaurants, music, galleries—all the happenings. Jim eyed the living room walls, crammed with art, half the works Doobie's. Art wasn't Jim's thing, but it had become Paco's passion just as intensely as Paco had become his. Paco pointed to the paper, a photo of a Doobie watercolor above the listings.

"*Por favor*, Chim, please, please, please." His dark eyes begged like a wounded cocker spaniel.

How could Jim say no to his little angel? That pouty bottom lip set Saturday night in stone.

* * * * * * *

Doobie arrived early on Saturday, as was expected of him, dressed in his usual beatnik black with a chip on his shoulder and six stiff drinks under his belt. Old habits die hard. He hated galleries.

He hated the politics and greed, the evil necessity of a process that devoured creative spirit. He hated openings most of all—having to chat up the common herd—answer the stupid questions of the pompous and pretentious uninformed. A night of pure bullshit and bombasity.

Big Jim Bullock and Paco were the first through the door. Jim headed for the wine bar as Paco flitted from painting to painting like a hyper kid at Toys R Us, gasping his admiration in a staccato of Spanish and English. "This one, this one_" he said, motioning Big Jim. Jim guzzled down the Merlot as he stood before the painting, the one in the newspaper—a trolley, a passing car, a bus. The colors were nice, bold. Purple against canary yellow. Red against blue. Not like the wispy, watery weak flowers painted by bored old ladies with nothing else to fill their empty lives. He liked Doobie's strength, his perfection. Paco had made a good choice, an accomplishment for a kid who's only exposure to art had been the graffiti that tagged the barrio. Jim was proud of him.

They flagged over Doobie, who was accustomed to their insistence of taking their purchases home immediately. First painting sold. They were so fucking easy. This odd couple had become good customers. The only ones he looked forward to seeing. They were rebels—Jim giving the system the finger at the same time he wore the systems uniform—Paco flaunting his fairyness in a macho universe. SF would've loved them.

Looking towards the door, Doobie saw the man standing there. Despite his immaculate "Tucson casual" clothes, Marco looked tough and greasy. Even seedy. The clothes did a poor job of hiding the man, who'd have looked more at home in cheap polyester. His demeanor was intimidating as piercing blue eyes darted from painting to painting. Instinctively, Doobie averted his eyes and headed for the wine bar, downing some Chablis to keep company with his stomach full of gin. Openings sucked worse than Tucson summers. More people streamed through the door.

As agitated as a junkie itching for his next fix, a gruff voice said, "I want this one." It was "Tucson casual," loudly summoning anyone who'd listen. Doobie walked over as the man pointed at the trolley painting.

"Sorry, it's sold," he said.

Marco drew attention to himself as he bellowed "I'll pay you double."

"It's sold," Doobie repeated, thinking:. One hell of a popular painting—should've done three.

"Triple." His eyes were menacing, glaring right through Doobie. Heads turned. Big Jim took two steps in their direction but the gallery owner got there first, diffused them both as tempers rose, reaffirmed the painting was unavailable. Seeing all attention focused on him, Marco stormed out the door. He hadn't meant to create a scene. Just the opposite. He knew he'd acted stupidly, but self-discipline had never been his strong suit. He just wanted the damn painting.

Doobie smiled. The night was looking up.

* * * * * * *

Big Jim Bullock was a pretty good cop. He should have noticed the car shadowing in the distance as he and Paco headed home.

Paco refused to retire until they found a spot on the wall for his latest acquisition, paid for by his mentor. Jim drove a nail in the wall and hung the damn thing even as he burned for bed, Paco's body and blow jobs.

* * * * * * *

The following night, Big Jim Bullock pulled into his driveway later than usual. Tucson's body count was climbing and the workload was overwhelming. They needed more cops to keep up with it, but the pay was lousy, way lower than the average, so there were few applicants. And most of them wouldn't have been hired anywhere else. They were a step or two above the perps they collared. At best.

Three drops of rain steamed from the windshield as Jim looked up at the dark house. It was unusual for the lights to be off. His cop-antenna rose. Cautiously he exited the car and put his key in the door. He turned on the light as he entered. Paco was on the living room floor, blood surrounding his lifeless form. All thoughts of forensics and not disturbing a crime scene left Jim as he knelt over Paco and cradled him in his arms. Tears streamed down Big Jim Bullock's face as he rocked his broken little sparrow.

He made the phone call. When the cops and forensics arrived, they found Jim sitting in a chair. All he could say was "why?"

Looking at the wall, he noticed a blank space where their latest Doobie had hung. Why, if it was a burglary, would someone take one painting and leave everything else? It made no sense. What was so special about that painting? That one little painting?

Then he remembered the grease ball at the gallery last night. How his anger took hold when he couldn't have that one painting. First thing next morning, Jim called the gallery. No, the creep hadn't signed the guest book. They were just glad to have ushered the lowlife out the door and end the disruption. The gallery owner was cooperative when Jim asked for Doobie's number.

* * * * * * *

Doobie opened the door and invited the cop in. He didn't like company. But Big Jim had called and there was desperation in the cop's voice. He needed to talk. They sat as Yoriko poured warm sake and cats marched across their laps.

"There's gotta be something about that painting. That was the only thing missing. I keep thinking about it, but in all honesty, I don't remember it that well. There was a trolley and a bus. Nothing out of the ordinary. Why was it important enough to kill for?"

Doobie couldn't figure it either. "Let's go to the computer," he said, "I always keep a copy on file." He booted up and clicked on the file. The painting came up clear as a bell. A trolley, a passing car, the ass end of a bus. Jim stared at it—trolley, bus, an old red

Chevy Lumina with the first three letters of the license plate. He saw the jewelry store in the background.

"The car. It's gotta be about the car," he said.

"Wait," Doobie said. "I have the photo I painted from filed too." He switched screens and pulled up the original photo.

"When did you snap that?" he asked.

"A week ago Saturday."

"The day of the jewelry store robbery."

He looked at the photo again. The license plate on the passing car was as clear as a soothsayer's eyes. Bingo.

Jim returned to the precinct and punched up the info on the license plate.

* * * * * * *

The red Lumina was parked in the driveway when the cops surrounded the house. Marco cowered inside, eyes flitting around the room, desperate for an exit route. Jim kicked down the door and tackled Marco when he tried to bolt. The painting was on the floor, leaning against the dining room wall. There was still jewelry from the heist scattered on the table next to some crack cocaine and an empty gun. Marco was bloodshot, weak and wasted. He gave up. It was over.

But not for Jim, who still held Marco in a hammerlock, yelling in his ear: "You dumb fucking junkie! You traded a couple years in the slammer for life—over this?" He looked over at the painting that had given his Paco such joy—and had cost him his life. Jim's eyes were blinded by tears, his brain blazed with rage. He tightened his forearm against Marco's neck, increased the pressure against his throat, made the weasel slobber like a St. Bernard as he gasped for mercy. It felt good. Too good.

He was going to kill the bastard.

"Back off, Jim" said another officer, pushing him off Marco. "This scumbag isn't worth it."

But he WAS worth it! Jim could have killed him in a heart-beat, laughing at the sound of cracking vertebrae as the man's life force drained from his worthless, ignorant body . But he heeded the other officer's words. He backed off.

It was the hardest damn thing he'd ever done.

Big Jim Bullock sighed as he stood in the dining room, staring at the painting with its blurred license plate, as the other officer cuffed Marco and led him to the squad car.

His beautiful Paco lay stiff and cold on a slab in the morgue.

It was all so unnecessary.

No one would ever have made the connection.

TUMBLEWEED

Charlie Blackhawk drove the silver 1979 Chevy Nova with his left hand on the wheel and his right hand around the cold can of beer planted between his legs. Its coolness against his thighs felt good. The small finger of his right hand absent-mindedly rubbed against his crotch as he hummed along to an old Waylon Jennings song on the radio.

Forty minutes had passed since Charlie had last seen another car along the deserted stretch of road. Too many trucks and too many drunks heading to or from Las Vegas. Instead, he had pulled off the main road at Jean, Nevada and was driving along the old secondary road that passed through Nipton on the California side. It was still morning and Charlie had already passed through Ivanpah, Cima, and Kelso. Now he was driving along an empty stretch of desert called the Devil's Playground. It's got a nice ring to it, Charlie thought to himself as he hummed off-kcy to a honky-tonk instrumental playing on the car radio. He planned to pick up U.S. 91 again when he reached Barstow to stop for gas.

Charlie felt himself getting hard beneath the Levis where his hand rested. He pulled his hand away, nearly tipping over the can of beer.

"I wasn't being bad, Momma. I wasn't doin' nothing bad." He spat out the words through clenched teeth.

Charlie pulled the Nova to the shoulder of the road, still mumbling to himself. He turned off the key and pushed open the door. He paced along the length of the car, uttering words that had meaning only to himself while he kicked the desert sand with his boots. Charlie was six-foot-one, tanned, and well-built. He had a rugged, outdoorsman look about him with a handsomely chiseled face.

This morning's beer was begging for release from Charlie's full bladder. Steam rose as he pissed a sunning lizard off its resting place on a rock.

Charlie laughed.

Paiute Wells was behind him.

That little hell-hole of a town had managed to bore him to death in less than a month. Nothing happened there and Charlie had become restless. It was time to find some action. He had been working his way back to California for the last three months, stopping off here and there to work for enough pocket money to keep him going.

It was time to head back for the cabin. He walked back to the car, guzzled the remaining beer, and threw the can to the floor.

He reached across the seat for his pack of Camel Filters, pulled one from the pack, and lit it. He drew the soothing smoke into his lungs, then exhaled as he turned the key in the ignition, stepped on the gas and returned to the road.

* * * * * * *

Driving along the desolate stretch of highway, Charlie's mind drifted like the desert sands from past to present and back again. It was a trick that his thoughts liked to play on him; taking him back, each time pulling ugly little pieces of that past and wedging them into the present. Sometimes Charlie drifted so deeply into the fogbank of mental trickery that he lost all concept of time and space. More often than not he was unaware of the retrogressions.

About three miles father down the road, Charlie spotted the twisted wreckage.

He slowed to forty, then thirty, then to a crawl as he pulled up behind the cars. They were a black Mercedes and an old Dodge and judging by appearances they must have hit each other head on. A New Mexico license plate hung loosely from the back bumper of the Mercedes. The front end was pushed in and the left fender was crushed against the Dodge.

There was a young woman slumped behind the wheel.

She was not moving.

As he walked up to the dented door on the driver's side he saw the blood trickling from her ear. One eye was partially dislodged from its socket.

He walked to the Dodge and looked inside. The man who had been driving was thrown to the passenger's side, his skull crushed where it must have slammed against the metal of the door.

He was dead.

Charlie returned to his own car and reached in for his keys. He walked around to the back and opened the trunk, pushing aside several license plates that lay among his clothing and other belongings. Removing a screwdriver from his tool kit he then walked around to the back of the Mercedes.

Crouching down, Charlie began to unscrew the license plate.

He heard a faint moan from inside the car.

Ignoring it, Charlie finished loosening the license plate, stood up and walked slowly back to his car. He whistled as he walked. He threw the license and the screwdriver into the trunk and walked over to the passenger side of the Dodge.

The door was jammed.

Charlie held the handle and pushed away from the car with his left foot while he pulled with all his strength on the handle. It finally gave way with a loud, creaking moan. The body fell, its arm and what was left of its head thudding to the ground.

Rifling through the man's pockets, Charlie finally found what he sought. He opened the wallet and counted the money that it held. Seventy-two dollars. Charlie took sixty dollars and pushed the wallet back into the dead man's pocket. He grabbed the corpse under the arms and lifted it back to the seat. Brains, like a spilled bucket of earthworms, oozed from the crushed cranium. The blood was already clotting. Charlie kicked the door shut with his boot and spat on the ground.

He walked over to the Mercedes and tried the door. It was locked. Humming and smiling as he walked to the other side of the car, he then tried the door on the passenger's side.

The door opened.

He heard the woman once more although she did not move.

"H...help...please," she stammered, almost inaudibly.

She was dying.

Charlie ignored her as his eyes searched the floor for her purse. He finally spotted it, sandwiched between the woman and the door. He grabbed a fistful of her hair and roughly pulled her head back. He reached across her slumping body and took the purse. He looked up at her face. One eyeball rolled loosely against her cheek. Blood continued to trickle from her ears as she moaned.

There was over seven-hundred dollars in cash along with several credit cards. He left the credit cards and took six-hundred and thirty dollars from the wallet.

"Stupid bitch," he muttered. "Didn't anyone ever tell you not to carry so much cash? Dumb, stupid cunt."

Charlie slid across the seat and was exiting the car when he spotted the small body in the back seat. It was a little girl about six or seven years old. Her neck was broken. She looked like a sleeping Girl Scout in the pale green dress that was rumpled above her thighs. She looked like his little sister, Lucy Mae. He opened the back door and slid in. He put his arms around her, lifting her limp body and holding her close to him. Her head fell back. He hummed a lullaby as he rocked her in his arms.

Charlie Blackhawk was crying.

He laid the little girl back on the seat and watched her with sadness. It was not two strangers Charlie saw in the Mercedes. His mind was focused on his mother, Wilma Blackhawk, and his beloved Lucy Mae. The past melted into the present, confusing Charlie's thoughts.

"You bitch!" Charlie screamed at the dying woman in the

front seat. "You've killed her! What kind of a mother are you? You rotten, drunken bitch!

"Lucy Mae, Lucy Mae," he wept.

Charlie's hand felt the soft green dress. It excited him. The fingers of his other hand toyed with the ruffle on her undies. "I miss you, Lucy," he whispered. "Please don't die." Gently, he removed the child's undies, rubbed them against his eyelids, then slipped then into his pocket.

Charlie sat up, leaned against the back of the seat and unzipped his fly.

It was time for the watching game.

That was when Charlie saw the car on the horizon.

The car that jolted him to the present with a thud. He judged it to be about five minutes away.

He reached for the handle on the car door. But the bitch in the front seat moaned. She was still alive. She was dying but she was still alive. What if she wasn't dead yet when the car reached the crash sight? What if she could talk?

No problem.

No problem at all.

Charlie's strong hands reached toward the front seat. He grabbed the woman firmly by her head.

It was as easy as killing a chicken for a Sunday picnic.

No problem at all.

He walked casually back to his Nova and started the engine. He adjusted the rear-view mirror and pushed the dark, curly hair from his forehead.

Charlie's eyes were as grey as frozen smoke.

His car took off. Swirling clouds of dust devils danced in its wake as it headed toward the gas stations and coffee shops of Barstow.

Charlie Blackhawk had worked up an appetite.

Be sure to look for more of Charlie Blackhawk in *Deranged: A Novel of Horror* by Lonni Lees, published by Borgo Press.

DADDY'S GIRLS

Dusk wrapped its dark cloak around the house as the preset exterior lights lit the front landscaping and driveway, adding an aura of warmth and welcome to the pathway that led to the front door. It was the picture postcard of deception, the pretty face that masked the darkness inside.

Mira Vistoso nestled comfortably in the southern California foothills like a spoiled cat settled on its velvet pillow. It rose above the valley, the smog, the traffic jams and dirt of the city below. Security gates protected it from strangers. Its narrow streets wound through the hillside, lined with million dollar tract homes crowned with terra cotta roof tiles, giving them a Mediterranean flair. The houses weren't large, but a million bucks didn't buy much in the golden state. All it bought was a fairly nice two-bedroom with a small family room off the kitchen, but it also bought a sense of security high on the green slopes above the clamor and graffiti; slopes that burned in the fire season and created rivers of mud in the rainy season and shook the foundations in earthquake season.

It was the American dream, California style.

One of the interior doors slammed so hard that the pictures on the girl's bedroom wall leaned askew on their nails, as though recoiling from the shock. One of the voices from the other room escalated to a high-pitched crescendo while the deeper voice remained a near whisper.

"She's at it again," said Megan, dark locks of straight hair whipping across her face as she shook her head in frustration.

She rose from where she sat on the floor and straightened the pictures for the umpteenth time. "Why is she always yelling?"

"Oh, all moms fight like that," said her eight year old little sister.

"That's not true at all, Jilly. Some mothers are nice. Some houses are quiet."

"Hah. How would you know that?"

"Because I'm four years older than you and I've been learning stuff since you were still eating your boogers, that's how I know."

"I don't believe you."

"When I have a sleep-over at Taylor's house her parents don't fight. They're nice to each other. And Taylor's mother tucks us in and kisses us goodnight."

"Really? Do you think our mom would do that?"

"Nope. One night I asked her. She said we were too old for that nonsense. But Jilly, I can't remember her ever doing that, even when we were little."

"Daddy comes and kisses us goodnight."

"That's because Daddy loves us."

"Doesn't mommy love us?"

"She sure doesn't act like it," Megan said, tousling her sister's golden curls as she sat down next to her on the floor. She leaned across and put her arms around Jilly, giving her a rib crunching bear hug. "I love you," she said. "You're the best little sister in the world."

Clomp. Clomp. Clomp. The heavy footfalls echoed down the hall. Clomp. Clomp. They got louder as they neared the girls' room. They both rose from the floor and sat side by side on Megan's bed, waiting for the door to open.

"She's wearing her angry feet again," said Jilly. "I hate when she stomps around like that."

The door flew open and their mother stood in the doorway. Allison was tall and blonde and might have been beautiful but for her permanent scowl. Megan could have sworn that those frown lines got deeper every day. Her mother was too young to have lines on her face. But there was always anger inside of her, waiting for any excuse to bubble up and explode. And it was beginning to show on the outside, like a subtle warning that you'd better watch out. As hard as she tried, and she had certainly tried, Megan could never figure out what her mother was so mad about. It was a permanent condition that could be set off by anything, whether it made any sense or not. Sometimes it was aimed at Daddy, who was pretty good at diffusing things, but when he wasn't around the girls took the brunt of it. Megan doubted that he knew they got punished so much, for unnamed crimes and misdemeanors they couldn't figure out, but they didn't tell him. They knew better. Telling would make things worse. She'd really explode then. Besides, her mother dared her once, telling her that husbands always sided with their wives, because they all loved their wives more than their children. Children, after all, were easily enough replaced. Megan doubted that this was really true, her mother said a lot of things that didn't seem right, but she wasn't going to take any chances. It wasn't worth the consequences.

"Take your baths and put on your jammies," said their mom. "It's time for bed." She turned and slammed the door, clomping her way loudly back down the hall.

There were times that Megan had thoughts that almost scared her, and she couldn't seem to stop them. She wondered if everybody had thoughts like that. They would surface every time their mother instigated a confrontation, every time Megan felt that she and Jilly were being treated unfairly, every time she heard her mother lay into Daddy for no reason at all. At those times fantasies would swirl around in her head, dancing their devil's dance. Mean thoughts. Dark and nasty ones. But, just like in scary fairy tales, she always managed to give them a happy ending. Maybe that made the thoughts okay, giving them happy endings.

"Sometimes I wish I could make her disappear," said Megan under her breath.

"You want to *disappear* her?"

"If I could. I've had a lot more years of her than you have and I'm worn out. I wish it was just you and me and Daddy," said Megan. "Wouldn't that be nice?"

Jilly thought for a minute, then said, "Do you think we'd be happier?"

"I know we would."

* * * * * * *

Daddy was more quiet than usual as the three of them sat at the breakfast table. He prepared the girls breakfast while Allison slept. She always slept in, and he never complained. It meant there was some modicum of peace at the beginning of the day. He got himself ready for work and got the girls ready for school and drove them to their destination on his way to the office. It was nice having uninterrupted time with them, but this morning the conversation would have a serious edge and he wasn't looking forward to it. As bad as things were with Allison he'd never seen it coming. Her refusal to go into marriage counseling should have given him a clue, his inability to please her in the simplest of ways should have given him a clue. He used to think he was doing something wrong, but he'd come to the realization that there wasn't a man on earth who could make her happy. He was no shrink, just a boring but successful businessman, but he'd finally come to a conclusion; she was just born with something crazy inside of her that gnawed away at her nerves like a shit house rat. Something about her was always broken and there was no magical Mr. Fix-It to make the repairs.

But he never saw *this* coming.

Megan noticed the suitcase in the back seat and her inquiry gave Daddy the opening he dreaded. "I won't be home tonight," he began, then paused and took a deep breath as though it might be his last. "I might not be home for awhile."

"Where are you going?" Megan asked.

"Your mother and I haven't been getting along and she felt we needed to be away from each other for awhile...."

"Daddy!" cried Jilly, "You can't just leave us. You can't! Let us come with you."

"I'll work it out, but it'll take time. In the meantime, I'll be seeing you every weekend. I promise. I'd never forget my angels."

"Why can't you just stay home?" asked Megan.

"When your mother gets an idea in her head there's no reasoning with her. It'll just take awhile before she cools down," he assured them, but his voice held no conviction. There was never any reasoning with Allison. There never had been. He'd been walking on egg shells since the day they said "I do." And playing the passive role of peacemaker never made it any better. He was ready to get their marriage annulled in the first three months but by then she was already pregnant. He'd thought when the girls came along things would be easier, but she carried the burden of motherhood like a martyr, as if her children were a punishment instead of a blessing. The girls, on the other hand, made his life easier, giving him a reason to weather Allison's storms. The car pulled up in front of the school. "We'll work it out," he repeated. "I promise."

The girls got out of the car, and Megan looked back at her father as he sat behind the wheel. There were tears in her eyes and she thought she saw tears in his.

"This really sucks," she said to him as she turned and walked away.

"You said a bad word," said Jilly, quickening her pace to keep up with her sister. "Suck is a bad word."

"There's a lot of words worse than that. And right now I want to say all of them."

"Better not. You'll *really* get in trouble."

"Not if you don't tell, I won't. Shit, shit, shit, damn! So there."

"Shit, shit, damn," repeated Jilly. "And, and—dog poop."

The girls held hands as they walked to the school gate, turning to watch their father's car as it drove down the street and away from them.

"I don't want to be alone with Mommy," said Jilly. "You

wanted to disappear her so we could be with Daddy, but she's disappearing him instead."

"She'll let us go with him, I'm sure of it Jilly. Why wouldn't she?"

* * * * * * *

That afternoon the school bus came to a stop at the entrance gate to Mira Vistoso. Megan and Jilly got off and started their uphill trek towards home. Tonight there would be no Daddy to kiss them goodnight, no Daddy to diffuse their mother's anger, no Daddy to make them feel safe and loved. But they still had each other. Megan loved her little sister and would give her all the love and protection that she deserved. And soon Daddy would be back home again to make it all better. Jilly was right. Megan had always dreamed of her mother somehow *going away* . Then she and her sister would live with their father and everything would be great. It never dawned on her that the opposite might happen—that Daddy would be the one to leave and they'd be stuck with their mother and worse off than ever.

They could hear the yelling before they reached the front door, their mother's voice at its usual shrill pitch. Was he already home? Megan's heart beat double-time in anticipation. But as they entered the house they could see her on the kitchen phone, pacing and damn near frothing at the mouth like some crazy pit bull on the attack.

Their hearts sank.

"No, you can't see them this weekend, or any weekend unless I decide you can. You're out of here for good and I'm in charge. You hear me? I'm calling the shots now, so just suck it up."

The girls tiptoed to the foot of the stairs.

"If you don't like it, then tell the lawyers." She slammed down the receiver.

Megan and Jilly scurried up the stairs and into their bedroom, closing the door behind them.

"She can't do that, can she?" Jilly sobbed. "I want my Daddy."

Megan hugged her close and said, "Don't worry, Jilly. I have a plan. Just let me think a minute."

But she didn't have a plan. Not yet. She sat there, silently, her thoughts slowly coming into focus. When she'd sleep over at her friend Taylor's house, they watched a lot of movies and old television shows that her parents would rent from Netflix. At home they were pretty well restricted to Disney movies, but at Taylor's house her parents treated them like grown-ups. They got to watch crime shows and old television shows like *Alfred Hitchcock Presents*. And they'd all sit and watch them together with a huge bowl of popcorn, just like she was family. Of course Megan never told her mother about the movies. That could well be the end of her sleep-overs. There was one episode of Hitchcock, Lamb to Slaughter, where the wife beat her husband to death with a frozen leg of lamb. She cooked the lamb in the oven, then fed it to the cop at her kitchen table, watching calmly as he ate the evidence. Could Megan do that? She thought about it and decided that it wouldn't work. Even if she could catch her mother off guard, which was unlikely, the police would know it was no accident. People just don't get their heads bashed in by accident. The cops wouldn't let up until they figured out who did it. She'd seen enough of those shows to know that cops look for motives and motives gave people away. And she had plenty of motive. No, she'd have to figure out something else.

Something that would look like an accident.

"What are you thinking about?" asked Jilly.

"Oh, nothing," Megan lied. As much as they disliked their mother, she was sure Jilly wouldn't approve of where her schemes were leading her. Jilly wasn't worldly like her big sister and hadn't been around long enough to know how truly awful things were. She didn't know there was anything else. And sweet as she was, she sure as heck couldn't come up with a solution. Besides, Megan's job was to protect her little sister from the bad stuff, even more so now that Daddy was gone.

* * * * * * *

The next morning Megan got up early. It was Saturday. Jilly was sound asleep in her bed and their mother wouldn't be up for hours. Saturday was laundry day and Megan had figured out how to make it the best washing and ironing day her mother would ever have. She tiptoed from the bedroom into the kitchen, leaving the lights off. She opened a kitchen drawer and felt around until she found a small steak knife. Holding it firmly in her grasp, she felt along the wall with her other hand until she came to the door that led to the half-basement. She turned the knob and opened the door slowly. Putting one foot down, she felt for the first step. Her toes felt for clothes scattered on the stairs. Her father called it "the lazy man's laundry chute" because they all had the habit of tossing dirty laundry down from the landing. Some of it would hit bottom, and some would remain scattered on the stairs. Slowly, feeling out one step at a time with her bare feet, she crept down the stairs, kicking items of clothing out of the way as she descended into the darkness. When she reached the bottom, she walked over to the laundry corner where the washer and dryer were located.

The first hint of daylight filtered through the small window, illuminating the ironing board just enough that she could make it out in the semi-darkness. It was set up near the washing machine. The iron sat atop the board, its cord hanging off the side and reaching to the floor. Ironing was one more chore her mother considered beneath her. It always provoking sighs and mutters, as if she were being chained in a dungeon. Well, the room did look a bit like a dungeon, she had to admit that. It was laced with cobwebs and smelled damp. Like in one of those old swashbuckler movies she'd watched at Taylor's house. Her mother spent Saturday morning chained there by that ironing cord and her own irrational thoughts. Megan wasn't going to waste any more time trying to figure her out. It was an unsolvable puzzle.

At least now she had a solution.

Megan lifted the cord and went to work, scraping the knife's sharp serrated edge along a section of the cord, slowly and carefully. It had to look like it was frayed from wearing out, not like it was cut. That would be a dead giveaway. About twenty minutes later she was satisfied with the result. She walked over to the small rinse sink, filled a cup with water, and poured it on the floor between the ironing board and the electrical outlet. Now all she had to do was wait.

Problem solved.

* * * * * * *

When Jilly woke up her sister was fast asleep in her bed.

By early afternoon the morning cartoons were over and the girls were bored. They watched as their mother gathered up the laundry for her afternoon of drudgery. Megan looked up at her and smiled. "Can Jilly and I go out for a walk? It's a beautiful day."

"Beautiful for you maybe," she replied with a sigh. "Go. Just go. I'm tired of having you under foot."

The girls were out the door before their mother could exhale another sigh. Or change her mind.

"Let's hike up the road and sit in the field," said Jilly. "That'd be nice."

By the time they reached the clearing they were out of breath. They flopped down on the grass, looked up at the clear blue sky and relished the silence. The only sounds were birds chirping and the hum from an occasional passing car. From here they could see the city below, with its tall buildings enveloped in a golden haze of smog and the freeway that snaked its way out of town. Jilly chattered like a magpie as her big sister told her stories. Megan told her that the clearing was their "laughing place", like in the old Uncle Remus stories. And it was. Anyplace but home was as welcome as two weeks at summer camp. But after a few hours in the field it was time to head back down the hill. And home.

"Let's pick wild flowers," said Jilly. "I'll bet Mommy will be really happy if we bring her flowers."

Megan knew that by the time they got home their dear mother wouldn't be anything at all. Just a crispy critter lying electrocuted on the basement floor. An unfortunate freak accident, like in the movies. But they gathered flowers until they could hold no more and headed back down the hill. Jilly hummed all the way home, looking forward to a smile from her mother. Megan knew it would take a heck of a lot more than a fistful of wild flowers. Experience had taught her that, but her sister was happy and she didn't want to spoil her mood. She loved when Jilly smiled, making laugh lines around those big blue eyes, round as marbles and full of innocence. She couldn't remember herself ever being that sweet. Not ever. They walked into the house—and silence. A good sign, thought Megan to herself. Ding dong, the witch is dead.

They entered the kitchen and fished through the cupboards until they found two vases in which to put the flowers. Megan wondered how long it would be before Jilly would notice their mother wasn't there. Should she let her go into the basement? Should she discover the body herself? They each filled the vases from the sink tap and arranged their displays. They held their vases out, admiring their handiwork.

"What kind of mess are you making now?" Said their mother as she stormed into the kitchen.

Megan nearly jumped out of her skin and her flowers crashed to the floor, shattering the vase. Shards of broken glass swam in the water as it spread across the floor. Her mother stomped over to where she stood and hit her in the face. Hard.

"What was that for?"

"If you're that jumpy you've got a guilty conscience about something."

"I didn't do anything."

"You always do something and that little love tap was for something you just didn't get caught for."

"It hurt."

"It's supposed to hurt."

"Look Mommy," said Jilly, trying to distract her. "We brought you pretty flowers."

Her mother looked at the flowers and said, "They have bugs on them."

* * * * * * *

When she had the opportunity, Megan went to the basement. By then the floor was dry but that wasn't the cause of her failure. The frayed cord didn't reach the floor. It arced from the ironing board to the electrical outlet, hovering about six inches from the floor and where the water had been waiting to do its job. Just six lousy inches.

It was time to come up with another plan.

Her mother liked to take long, leisurely baths on Sunday afternoons. Enter plan two. When her mother was downstairs, Megan sneaked into the master bathroom and looked around. The shelves were filled with expensive perfumes, boutique bath salts—and bath oils. Lots of bath oils. She picked up a bottle that had been previously opened and recognized the aroma. It smelled like her mother. She wrinkled her nose and walked over to the tub, uncapping the bath oil. She poured some into the tub, smearing it around the bottom and sides until she was satisfied there was enough to do the job. Slip. Fall. Bump head. Get dead. By tomorrow their nightmare would be over once and for all.

She heard the phone ring and could hear her mother's voice yelling from downstairs. From what she was saying Megan knew she was on the phone with Daddy again.

"I changed the locks, so don't even try to come over here. And don't ever again try to call the girls. They don't want to talk to you."

What a liar.

Then a moment of welcome silence.

"I'm going to have your cell phone number blocked, how do you like that?"

And she slammed down the receiver.

When the phone rang again she didn't answer it, just let it ring and ring and ring, like a futile plea from the other end of the wires.

"Shut up," Allison screamed, holding her ears. "Just shut the fuck up."

Megan could hardly wait for Sunday. Her mother was tightly wrapped in mean and nasty. She hurt Jilly and she hurt Daddy and she enjoyed every minute of it. Megan didn't mind so much when *she* got hurt, she was tough and could handle it. But it broke something deep inside of her when she saw her mother hurt the people she loved. It just wasn't right and it sure wasn't fair and it had to stop. It was her job to stop it. And she needed to end the rage building inside of her once and for all. She didn't want it there. She didn't want to feel that way. It was something her mother put there and she wanted it out. She didn't want to end up like her mother, hating the world and taking it out on everybody else. She just wanted some peace. And she wanted her father back. Sometimes you just do what you have to do, she told herself. And that night she slept like a baby.

* * * * * * *

Sunday afternoon Megan and Jilly sat on the floor of their bedroom, the Monopoly board between them. The house was unusually quiet and their mother had distanced herself from them all morning, leaving them to play, undisturbed. The girls had prepared sandwiches for lunch and had taken them to their room. Jilly nibbled on her peanut butter and jelly sandwich as they played, smudging jelly on her game piece and onto some of her Monopoly money. Megan's sandwich sat on a plate beside her, uneaten. She was too excited to eat. Today was the day they'd get their father back and everything would be right. Today was the day their mother would take her final exit.

"The quiet is almost scary," said Jilly. "I keep waiting for her to explode through the door."

But she didn't.

Megan smiled when she heard the water running into the bathtub down the hall.

"She's taking her bath now," she said. "She'll be in there for hours."

"Good." Jilly moved her game piece and landed on Park Place. "I'm buying it," she said, triumph in her voice as she counted out her money.

The water stopped flowing into the bathtub and Megan listened, waiting for the final thump.

And it came.

Followed by a stream of obscenities. "Goddamn sonofabitch! Jesus fucking Christ!"

"What was that?" said Jilly, rising from the floor and racing towards her mother's room, Megan following behind her.

Jilly opened the door to the master bath, "Mommy? Are you okay?"

"No, I'm not okay," said her mother. She was sitting in the tub rubbing her ankle. "I slipped on the damn bath oil. You'd think at twenty dollars a bottle...."

"Do you want me to help you?"

"No, I'll be okay. Just leave me alone so I can enjoy my bath," she said. "Damn, my ankle hurts. And my hip. And damn near everything else."

"Are you sure?" said Megan, "I could...."

"I just want to sit here in the warm water. It'll help," she said. "Now just go away and leave me in peace."

Shit, thought Megan as they left the room, the bitch has more lives than an alley cat.

* * * * * * *

Monday morning the girls awoke to the sound of their alarm clock. There would be no father at the breakfast table so Megan took charge. They took off their jammies and put on their school clothes. Megan picked up their jammies and gathered their clothes from the previous day and carried them downstairs to the kitchen. She opened the door to the half-basement and tossed them down, then turned back into the kitchen to make them some breakfast.

"It was kinda nice not hearing Mommy stomping around yesterday. I guess it's hard to make so much noise when you're limping," Jilly said, then added: "But I'm sorry she hurt herself."

"Yea, she was hopping around like a one-legged tap dancer," Megan smiled.

"Can we call Daddy?" Jilly whispered, afraid her mother might somehow hear her, even though she was fast asleep in her bed.

"Mommy fixed it so we can't."

"We could call him at work."

"He's not there yet, it's too early."

"We could leave him a message. We could tell him we miss him."

Megan reached for the wall phone and dialed, then punched in her father's extension and handed the phone to her sister.

"Hi Daddy, this is Jilly. I miss you Daddy, when are you going to come for us?" She was starting to cry, so Megan took the phone from her.

"Daddy, we love you and Mommy lied. We want to see you so bad. We'll try to call again when we can. I love you." And she hung up.

* * * * * * *

At 3:15 in the afternoon the school bus pulled up at the gate to Mira Vistoso and the girls climbed down and out of the bus, carrying their backpacks full of books and homework. Jilly held one piece of paper in her hand. She waved it in the air as they headed for home.

"Mommy will be happy," she said. "I got a gold star."

"I'm very proud of you, Jilly. You're so smart." Megan always said the words she knew Jilly wouldn't hear from their mother. "You're going to grow up to be somebody really important, maybe even the president."

"You really think so?" Her blue eyes shone with delight.

"Oh, I know so. I know lots of stuff."

When they entered the house Jilly ran from room to room, the paper with the gold star in her hand, looking for her mother. "Mommy, Mommy, I've got something to show you." But her mother wasn't in the kitchen, or the family room, or in the living room. "Mommy?"

"Maybe she went somewhere," said Megan.

Jilly ran through the kitchen and opened the door that led to the garage. "Her car's here," she said. "Her car's right here in the garage." She went back into the kitchen. "I'll go look upstairs, maybe she's taking a nap or something." And she ran upstairs, gold starred paper in hand.

Megan saw her mother's purse sitting on the kitchen counter, where she always left it. An uneasiness swept over her. She opened the door which led to the half-basement and that's when she spotted her mother lying at the foot of the stairs, at the bottom of the lazy man's laundry shoot. She wasn't moving, so Megan started down, kicking away the few items of clothing that remained scattered on the steps. She saw her own pajama bottoms that had somehow twisted around her mother's ankle and caused her to lose her balance, hurling her down into the darkness. Her mother was cold to the touch and she wasn't breathing. Her immediate thought was, *it's about time.* But then the reality of it slapped her in the face harder than her mother ever had. She was looking down at a dead person. White skin, blue lips, stiff fingers reaching upward. Wishing her mother dead was one thing, but seeing the reality of her cold, bruised body was something else. It was ugly. And it was final. A lot more final than just wishing her to go away to some nameless place beyond her reach. A part of her was relieved, a part of her horrified. Megan ran back up the stairs as fast as she could, slamming the door behind her, heart pounding.

"Mommy's not in her room," said Jilly as she walked into the kitchen. "What's the matter Megan, you look funny. Like you're gonna throw up or something."

"We have to call 911. And we have to call Daddy."

"What happened?"

"She fell down the basement steps."

"Is she okay?" Jilly started towards the basement door but her sister stopped her.

"I think she's dead."

* * * * * * *

By the time Daddy got to the house, the cops and paramedics and crime scene investigators were already there. Questions were asked and answered and asked again. Photographs were taken. Allison was finally taken away, covered in a white sheet. It wouldn't take long for them to verify their first impression— she was the unfortunate victim of an accidental fall down the stairs. A lot of accidents happened in one's own house. She was just one more statistic.

Megan and Jilly and their father sat at the kitchen table for a long time, exchanging comments over the tragedy, but none of them seemed as sad as they should be. Each one tried to hide the relief they felt while they said all the right words and hugged each other and managed a tear or two.

As the two girls headed upstairs for their bedroom, Jilly said, "I'm so glad Daddy's back. I missed him." Then, half way up the steps, she stopped her sister. At first she seemed perplexed, then, looking straight into her eyes, she asked: "Did you push her?"

"Of course not. We were at school. They said she was—they said that it happened hours ago."

"But she disappeared, just like you wished for." She looked at her big sister, awe and admiration on her face. "It's like you've got some kind of magic."

"No, sometimes accidents just happen."

And, hand in hand, they ascended the stairs.

POSSUM

Jolene was young but she'd already given up on any childish dreams of a better life. Life just didn't get better in these parts, and she knew the sooner she accepted that fact the sooner she could deal with the reality and monotony of day to day survival. Her momma had somehow figured it out, and her momma before her, so how hard could it be? And why didn't any of them pass the secret of it all down to her? Being her husband's punching bag sure as hell hadn't been the reality she'd bargained for, but that was the truth of it, bruises and all. And it wasn't like he hit her every day anyway, only when she was asking for it. Only when she got out of line. She just had to figure out where that line was and learn not to cross it. But the line kept changing, like the shoreline at Black Cedar Lake in the sweltering heat of summer.

The house was a cracker-box, cloned with a million others during the optimistic post-war boom that spread across the country. The progress seemed to have spread everywhere but here, except for the few houses that were erected for returning soldiers to buy cheap upon their return from battle. The kitchen, a time-worn poster child frozen in the 1950s, wore broken pink tiles and faded linoleum floors. Jolene Crowder stood at the kitchen sink, staring through the broken window pane as she scraped off last night's crusted dishes. The bruised clouds that hung in the morning sky matched the marks that ran up her left arm, blue and grey and angry.

Jolene eyed the beat-up travel trailer parked at the back edge of the yard. Looking like a silver turtle with a humped back, it hid in the shadows of turning autumn trees along the railroad tracks. Hard to believe two people could have lived in that, much less one person on a good day. But you do what you gotta do. She was less trapped than when she and Beau lived in that can of dents, but she felt trapped nonetheless. Their home, if one could call it that, had sat at the back of Ma Crowder's place. She guessed Ma Crowder wasn't too bad for an in-law. Not too bright, as things go, but she seemed okay and never gave them a hard time about anything. At least Ma'd given them a place to camp when Beau had shown up with his knocked-up teenage bride. Back then it was just Beau and her and a kitchen full of meth fumes. About six months along she'd convinced Beau the smells weren't good for her—and sure as hell wouldn't do once the kid arrived. "If I wasn't cookin' meth we'd still be living off Moon Pies and RC Cola," he'd reminded her. It took a lot of begging on her part and a lot of hitting on his, but he finally rented them a real house. It was the only battle she'd ever won. Her only victory in a war she knew she'd never win. It was still in Hooper's Holler, just up the road a piece. She figured it was likely the last right thing he'd do for them, but at least it was something. He'd towed the tin can into their new yard, and set up his lab while Jolene tended the baby and the house. It was the only order in her life. She wondered how life might have come out if she hadn't been knocked up at fifteen with no way out. She was likely headed to being a grandma by the time she hit thirty, like most every other dumb kid in the Holler. It was their legacy, handed down from one generation to the next, like an old family bible or a set of chipped dishes.

Thinking on it wasn't gonna change weeds into rose bushes. Hooper's Holler sat at the edge of nowhere, populated by bad teeth and bad choices, with nowhere to go and no way to get there. In Pappy's day the hills were filled with stills and shotgun fire, while her generation had replaced them with meth labs and Saturday Night Specials. That's all the progress they knew and likely all they'd ever know. But the folks there in the Holler were built strong and stubborn as pit bulls and played the hand they were dealt as best they knew how.

"Maaaaaa!"

Jolene pivoted around at the sound of her baby's wail.

"Faw down, go boom," he whimpered, sprawled across the linoleum.

She walked over and picked him up, held him close as his bottom lip jutted out and quivered. "Poor baby," she said. "Possum go boom and mama make better." She held his face close to hers and covered it with noisy kisses. "Mama kiss Possum's whiskers," she repeated until he started to giggle.

"Tickle," he laughed.

She carried him across the kitchen and lowered him into the high chair, kissing him gently on the top of his head, then mussed his sandy curls before heading to the stove. By the time she'd walked across the room his chin was resting on his chest and he was dead asleep. Jolene figured when you're birthed into the eye of a hurricane you learn to sleep anywhere, anytime. Her sweet little Possum made it all worthwhile—the beatings, the nasty words, all of it. She removed six strips of bacon from the fridge, placed them in the cast iron skillet and lit the propane.

The kitchen door opened with a crash.

Beau, scrawny and pale, wore an ugly sneer as he entered the room. He was wiry but he was tougher than a box of nails—and she had the marks to prove it. His eyes were wild and bloodshot and darted around the room in a paranoid dance. Jolene froze in place, knowing too well what was coming. He was strung out and she was his target—the convenient dog that got kicked in it's owner's frustration, taking its licks in exchange for a moment of kindness.

But that moment never came with Beau.

The bacon sizzled on the stove, its sweet aroma mixed with the all too familiar scents of fear and rage. He'd been out back for three days, using up half the profits from the lab and twitching like a toad in hot water. Jolene held her breath, flipped the bacon strips, turned off the stove.

"Don't you be turning your back on me, bitch," he said. "Show some respect."

Silence.

"You hear me?"

She turned and faced him.

"Yes, Beau. Sorry, Beau."

"Don't sound to me like you got your heart in it." He walked up to her, grabbed her wrist, twisting it until he saw the pain in her eyes. "Got yer attention now, Sweet Pea?"

"Yes," she said, looking at the crazy in his eyes. "Breakfast?"

"Not that pig slop. Sweet Jesus, Jolene, some good cooking ain't much to ask."

The game had begun. Guessing what he really wanted. Afraid to guess wrong. It always started the same, him expecting her to read his scrambled mind. Scared of making a misstep. But he stacked the cards carefully before he ever started to play. She wondered what she'd ever seen in him, but he was different then. Or so she'd thought at the time. He was older by a few years and seemed so grown up and cock sure of himself. He'd charmed her 'til she didn't know if she was on foot or horseback and he had her flat on her back quicker than a fly on molasses.

"Stop it, Beau, please."

There was an edge to her voice he didn't like. There was always something he didn't like. A word. A look she'd give him. A question. Anything at all could set him off.

"You're a whole lotta mouth and no listen," he said, then accentuated it with a strong gut punch that knocked the wind out of her.

"Look at this," he said, pointing around the room. "You made me a prison. I'm stuck in hell with you and that little bastard there and I don't reckon he's even mine. First time you did me it was like you'd been doin' it for a living. You didn't fool me, you whore, tricking me by getting knocked up by who knows who and then blamin' me."

"You know better'n that." He'd known damn well he was her first, but she'd put her all into it, trying to please him, trying to be romantic and passionate like in those paperbacks with the lusty cover art that she sneak-read under the covers. But the act was over practically before it started. Not like in the books at all. He was more like a pig rutting in a hollow than some knight in armor. And there were no fancy, romantic words like when he first started to pursue her. Now he was getting what he wanted and he didn't tell her she was pretty or he loved her or none of that. About the best he'd said as he undressed her was that she was scrawny but her hips were built for birthin' babies. And to top it all, her friends had said you can't get pregnant the first time you do it. Well, her friends were wrong.

"And keep your voice down afore you wake up Possum," she said. Too firmly? Too much like an order? That was asking for it. She took two steps backward, distancing from his glare, just beyond his arm's reach.

"You start doing drama, we're gonna have a "come to Jesus" meeting. You're ready to meet Jesus, ain't you Jolene?"

He lunged forward. A hard fist to the jaw shut her up. Another in her stomach got her attention. His arms swung at her faster than a jackhammer on cement until she begged him to stop. "I've just begun," he said. "I'm gonna put a whole lotta hurt on you until you learn. Shit, I'm gonna kill you and that soul-sucking little bastard you stuck me with and then I might just go and kill somethin' else just for the fun of it."

Possum woke up to the sounds of his momma and daddy arguing. He whimpered. His whimpers escalated into high volume wails, piercing the room.

"Shut the fuck up!" said Beau, "Shut the damn kid up or...."

He knew how to push her buttons. She hated the "F" word, but she wasn't going to take the bait.

"Calm down," she said in a whisper. "You know it's just the meth talkin'."

He slapped her.

Possum howled.

"I said shut the fuck up." He turned from Jolene and faced his son.

Possum raised his arms, reaching out as Beau walked over to the high chair. Jolene lifted the cast iron frying pan from the stove, its handle hot in her hands, and before she could form a lucid thought slammed it into the back of Beau's head. Bacon grease flew, hitting the walls and puddling on the linoleum. Beau hit the floor with a thud and lay there motionless. She whacked him five more times for good measure, each whack harder and with more determination than the last. Something inside her had snapped. It was one thing to slap the dog mess out of her, but she wasn't going to let him start on abusing her little Possum.

Jolene had finally found the line she couldn't let him cross.

She looked down at the floor. Beau didn't move. He just lay there on the ugly green linoleum forgetting to breathe. She stood there looking down at him for a long time. Waiting for him to stir, waiting for him to rise up and take his revenge. But he didn't move. Not one bit. There was a smile on her face, an expression of triumph. She felt better than she'd felt in a long, long time. And she didn't feel scared any more.

"Trapped, Beau?" she said, giving him a hard kick to the ribs. "Trapped? How do you think I feel?" A hard kick to the side of his head. "Ain't nobody between Hooper's Holler and hell more trapped than me—and that's saying a lot, don't you think?"

Possum was laughing as Jolene lifted him from the high chair.

"Dada go boom."

"Sure did, Possum."

"Mama kiss him whiskers, make all better?"

Beau's body lay motionless on the floor, silent and bloody and covered in bacon grease. It was the best he'd looked in a long time.

"Nah, he's just fine," she said. As she stepped over Beau she bent down and picked up two strips of bacon from the floor, then handed them to Possum as she lifted him out of the high chair.

* * * * * * *

Possum was still chewing on the bacon as she bundled him and headed out the back door, carrying him in her arms. There was a cold bite in the air and a colder one that shot through her clear down to the bone. Life was bad but she never imagined it could get this bad. Killing Beau was the last thing she'd have thought of. It just happened—she was only defending herself and her baby boy—but who'd believe her? Certainly not Beau's own ma, but there was no place else to go. The last time she saw her own folks was when she'd told them she was in a family way. That was a bad day, followed by many more bad days. Her life had become one long string of bad days. She remembered the disappointment in her mother's eyes, the rage in her father's. He had her bag packed and booted her out the door faster'n a fox flying through a hen house. She'd shamed him, for sure, but not as bad as she'd shamed herself. On the up side, he had one less mouth to feed. That door was closed forever.

Brown leaves scattered along the railroad tracks like dead frogs or dried up dog shit, crunching under foot as they headed down to Ma Crowder's place.

* * * * * * *

Jolene banged on the torn screen door with her free hand, perching Possum against her hip with the other. The radio show Voice of Redemption blared from within the house. She knocked again, harder this time. Chickens scattered from the porch, flapping their wings and clucking in alarm.

"Hold yer horses," came a voice from inside. "Keep yer britches on." Ma Crowder placed her knitting needles and yarn onto the side table and rose, with effort, from her easy chair. The chair was covered in faded floral, frayed and tired and old. The wallpaper on the living room walls was even more faded, with water marks from where the roof had leaked over the years, and edges that had long ago peeled loose, their corners folded down like some sad dog's ears. Old family photos hung on the walls from cheap frames. Photos of young children smiling, their eyes full of hope and pictures of parents and uncles and grand-mothers with empty eyes devoid of any of the optimism they may have held in their youth. Some of them had shoulders bent from the weight of life, while others held their shoulders square and proud like nothing in the world could wear them down. Needlepoint flowers were mounted in frames along side the photos, each stitch sewn painstakingly by Ma Crowder herself to add splashes of cheer to her humble home. She saw God's flowers as happy gifts, free to even the poorest of his children, and surrounded herself with them. On the walls, on the uphol-stery, in vases filled with plastic roses that would never die. Even her well-ironed housecoat was scattered with a lavender and purple floral design. The room itself held the stale, musty aroma of old furniture and the faint dampness of last springs rain showers that had seeped into the walls, but the widow Crowder always kept the place clean and well dusted. She took pride in her home and always kept it presentable should there be an unexpected visitor, or just for herself when she woke up in the morning and could see the results of a job well done. Her heavy form made its way to the door and opened it, motioning Jolene inside.

"Good Lord, child, where's the fire? And what in mercy happened to your face?"

"Ma," was all that came out, raspy as a bull frog. "Ma...."

When Possum saw Ma Crowder his eyes lit up like a K-Mart Blue Light Special. "Meemaw," he squealed, reaching out for her. Ma Crowder took Possum from his mother and snuggled him against her chest as she crossed the room and turned off the radio. Her little grandson was the light of her life, so blonde and white and pink and innocent. He took after her side of the family and looked the spittin' image of her Beau when he was a wee'un himself.

"Take a sit," she motioned to Jolene as she returned to her easy chair and eased herself down, positioning Possum on her lap. "Sit," she repeated, pointing to the straight backed chair across the room.

Jolene sat.

"Your face is all bloody and bruised, child, now tell me what happened."

Jolene just stared at her, not knowing where to start—afraid to say what she knew she must. Instead, she pushed up the arms of her sweatshirt, exposing more cuts and bruises. Blue, purple, green and yellow, all in different stages of healing. "It never stops," she whispered.

The room was silent.

"He was gonna kill me and Possum both," she finally managed.

"Dada go boom," said Possum.

"Why the hell didn't he come with a warning sticker?" Jolene sighed. "He was so strung out on that damn meth that he was trying to kill us. It's been bad, Ma, but it ain't never been as bad as this."

"Well," said Ma Crowder, "that's a hard one to swallow... that's my beau yer talkin' about." Then, as an afterthought, she added, "And watch your language around Possum." But as she looked at the bruised girl her heart knew it was true. She might have closed her eyes to a lot when her son was growing, but she knew he was no angel. "The good Lord says woman must obey her husband," she said, almost to herself. "But he also says a wife is to be honored—and there ain't nothing honorable about knocking you into next Tuesday." Ma Crowder let the thoughts form in her mind before she spoke again. "Child, there ain't nothin' in this world gets so broke you can't somehow fix it." She hugged Possum, who had fallen asleep in her lap.

"My biggest mistake was not walking in the other direction first time I ever laid eyes on him. But he charmed me, Ma. He charmed me something awful. How was I to know what I was gonna be in for?"

"Life's full of mistakes, Jolene. Every one of us makes mistakes—that's why God made those little erasers at the end of pencils. Ain't nothing done can't be fixed, one way or the other."

"I killed him."

Jolene's words hit Ma like a sledgehammer on an egg shell. In that same instant, an engine's roar broke the morning silence as a truck fish-tailed into the yard, stirring up clouds of dust in its wake as it sped across the gravel drive. Jolene snapped her head around and looked out the window. The pick-up came to a screeching halt just feet from the house. Beau's truck. The engine died with a cough and a sputter. The truck door opened, and there he stood, bloody and full of madness and, unfortunately, very much alive.

He held a gun in one hand, his other hand clenched into a fist that turned his knuckles white. The pupils in his eyes were black pinpoints, the whites were filled with flaming red rage. He focused on the front door and strode in their direction, waving the gun and growling like a wounded grizzly.

Jolene forgot to breathe for what seemed like forever. Then she gasped.

"He's gonna kill us," she said. "He's gone bug-shit crazy. Hide Ma, please hide Possum. Don't let him find Possum."

"Now, now, I can reason with my boy," Ma Crowder said, but even as the words came out she was rising from her chair to head out of the room. She held Possum with one arm and grabbed her knitting with her free hand and headed for the bedroom. Possum stirred from his slumber as she glanced around the room, then headed for the bedroom closet.

"Meemaw," he said, yawning.

"Shhh, Possum," she said as they edged into the closet, "we're playin' Go Hide and Seek and we gotta be real quiet, okay?"

"Otay." He smiled up at her as she lay him on a pile of clothes in the corner of the closet floor, then he fell back asleep. Ma Crowder settled in next to him, trying to hold her breath as she heard the front door crash open.

"Fucking bitch!"

"Now, Beau—you just calm down now."

"You and Possum's nothing but a curse on me." His face was

twisted with a hate stronger than she'd ever seen before. "Where the fuck is he?"

"Gone. He's gone. Your mama took him down to the Hooper's General to get him some sweets. He ain't here, Beau."

"You lie, that's all you ever done is lie and lie and then lie some more."

"I'm truthin' you, Beau. Honest to God I swear I am."

Ma Crowder listened from the closet as Beau ranted and raved. He sounded a lot like her late husband. The yelling, the threats, the hitting. Ma's old man could pass out hurt like candy corn on Halloween. All Beau's life she'd given her son the benefit of the doubt, but he was his father's son after all. What else could be expected? That was pretty much all he'd seen growing up and his legacy had come home to roost. She couldn't blame *him*, not really. But he, sure as God was in heaven, wasn't going to hurt her sweet little Possum. Not knowing what else to do, she picked up her knitting and started knitting in the dark. Her knitting always eased her mind and when she was done there was always something to show for it—oven mitts, toaster cozies, little hats for Beau, fancy little coasters—her house was filled with more knit goodies than a big city thrift store.

"He ain't here, Beau."

"Get your hands off me," he yelled. "I'm gonna find that little bastard here somewhere."

Then Ma Crowder heard the gun shot.

The house was quiet except for the sounds of Beau racing through the hallway, opening and slamming doors along the way. She held her breath when she heard the door to her bedroom open. She heard his footfalls across the bare wood floor, coming nearer to their hiding place. Quietly as she could, without making noise or disturbing her sleeping grandchild, she rose to a standing position just as the closet door flew open.

"Aha, found y'all," Beau said with a crazy smile, aiming the gun into the shadows. Ma Crowder's hands flew forward and Beau stumbled backwards, screaming. He reeled, spun in circles, fell against the bed, rose again—all the while flailing his arms and grasping at the knitting needles embedded in both his eyes. His hands felt the walls until he found the doorway and stumbled toward the living room—and Jolene.

Ma Crowder looked down and saw Possum was still asleep, so she exited the closet and cautiously followed her son into the other room.

Jolene was lying on the floor, sweatshirt covered in blood, slowly moving towards consciousness as Beau stumbled around the room.

"Wha' wha...Maaa," was all that came out of his mouth. His arm hit a lamp and the gun as well as the lamp fell to the floor with a crash. Jolene reached for the gun, grabbed it, rose shakily to a standing position and aimed it at Beau.

Despite her shaking hands, she zeroed in on her target and pulled the trigger. The recoil knocked her legs out from under her and she fell to the floor as the reek of gun powder filled her nostrils and mixed with the stale aroma of the room.

Beau had been harder to stop than a brakeless semi truck careening down a steep mountain road. But Beau's own bullet in his head put him out of his misery and put Jolene out of hers as well. Beau had stopped ranting—stopped hitting—stopped breathing. Once and for all. He dropped to the floor with a hollow thud and lay there with a hot bullet in his cold brain and knitting needles jutting out of his eye sockets like straws sticking out of a Big Gulp soda from Hooper's General Store.

Amen.

Ma Crowder walked across the room and knelt next to Jolene. She was still alive. Ma checked her wound. It was nothing more than a bullet hole in her shoulder, so a bit of fixin' and stitchin' and she'd be just fine. Ma went into the hall closet, got out her sewing kit, and went to work.

Getting Beau's dead body into the bed of the truck was no easy task but they got the job done. The two women had dragged his dead weight through the cinders and the dandelions and the nettles and the flapping wings of scattering chickens. And they had somehow managed to muster the strength ,after three failed attempts, to hoist him up into the bed of the beat up old truck. Jolene's shoulder hurt like hell and Ma Crowder was panting like a hound dog in the midsummer sun.

"Well, now ain't it just amazing what two women can accomplish when they stick together and put their hearts into something." Ma Crowder was gasping like a fish out of water, as she tried to catch her breath, her mouth opening and closing as it formed little circles.

"But now what?" asked Jolene. "We've gotta be in a shit-load of awful here."

"Go to the house and get Possum," said Ma with authority. "We've still got plenty of work to do. We might be poor women here in the Hollow, and we might not have much power in the scheme of things, but we stand strong and we stand up for our own. And you are my own, Jolene, just as sure as if I'd given birth to you myself." She paused to take a breath. "Now stop yer fretting and go get Possum."

* * * * * * *

By the time they pulled up to Beau and Jolene's place Possum was wide awake.

"Take him into the house child." said Ma Crowder. "We got some work that needs doing."

Jolene took her baby into the house and lowered him into his high chair. Then with shaking hands she spread some saltine crackers onto the tray in front of him. It would keep him occupied while she went back outside to help Ma Crowder with whatever she had in mind regarding the dead body of her husband. She wondered how they were ever going to get out of this mess. It was Beau's mess and once again she was going to have to clean up after him. Just this one last time.

By the time she got outside Ma had driven the pick-up all the way back to the old travel trailer that served as Beau's meth lab. She lowered the truck's gate and yelled out to Jolene as she was walking across the yard toward her. "Get a move on, girl, I need me a hand here."

Pulling Beau out of the truck was easier than putting him in. But dragging him into the trailer took all the strength the two women could muster. Jolene was scared, but not as scared as every day of her life had been since she'd become Beau's. It was looking like she'd just traded one hell for another, wondering how in the world she could explain away a dead husband with a bullet in his head.

The hinges creaked as Ma opened the door to the trailer and walked inside. The stink of meth fumes forced her to cover her mouth and nose as she walked across the room and took a beer bottle from the counter top. Her eyes were burning as she emptied the dregs into the filthy sink and walked back out the door, bottle in hand, and into the welcome of daylight. The clouds were finally dissipating and rays of sunshine held the promise of a lovely afternoon. She filled the empty beer bottle with gasoline from the red can that sat outside the trailer door. Jolene just stood there as Ma went back inside and stuffed a wiping rag into the neck of the bottle. She walked back outside and stood next to her daughter-in-law.

"What are you doing, Ma?" She said, eying the bottle in the older woman's hand.

"You're just a young-un, Jolene, so there's things you might not know about the Holler. There's those that do wrongs that just can't be made right no other way. So sometimes "accidents" happen. Like there's a hunting accident, or somebody might fall off Beaudry's Cliff—or one more meth lab might just blow up. Things like that happen all the time and they just ain't nothing anybody looks into too closely."

Jolene remembered how Ma Crowder's man had accidentally shot himself, right in their own back yard. How Ma had said it happened when he was cleaning his gun. Nobody had ever questioned it—not Beau—not the sheriff—not Jolene when she heard the story. And Ma was right about the meth labs—they blew up all the time. Just one more unfortunate accident in Hooper's Holler.

"Hand me them matches," said Ma. "We've got a little more work to do." Ma looked at the bottle in her hand and smiled. "Time for a bit more education, Jolene." Ma stretched out the next words slowly, as if she were trying to teach the ABC's to a mentally challenged young child. "This here's called a Molly... toff Cocktail," she said, raising the bottle to accentuate her statement. "I hear'd the Russians invented it. So's I guess them dirty pinko commies were good for at least something."

Jolene watched as Ma walked over and faced the open door of the trailer and lit the match, holding it against the rag until it ignited into a slow burning flame. Jolene figured she sure had underestimated her mother-in-law. While Jolene's heart was nearly pounding out of her chest, the older woman appeared as calm as the surface of water on a soft spring morning. Then Ma Crowder tossed the flaming beer bottle through the door with the strength of a pitcher on the mound, and they both ran toward the house faster than coons being chased by hungry hounds.

By the time they reached the back door the trailer blew up with an explosion that shook the ground. Glass flew, the pick-up burst into flames, and the tips of tree branches recoiled from the heat. Pieces of metal flew through the air every which way as the two women walked into the house.

"Now let's clean up this mess," said Ma as she looked at the grease and blood on the kitchen floor.

"Dada go Boom," said Possum.

ABOUT THE AUTHOR

Lonni Lees has had several of her short stories published in *Hardboiled Magazine*, where she is a regular contributor. Her stories have also appeared on ezines *Yellow Mama* and *Einstein's Pocket Watch*, as well as in the anthology *Deadly Dames*. Stories will be coming out shortly in the anthologies *More Whodunits* and *Battling Boxers*. Her first novel, *DERANGED*, is published by Borgo Press.

She won awards for writing as well as for her art. In the past she did illustrations for books as well as the *L.A. Mensa Journal*. Her artwork accompanies several stories by other writers in *Yellow Mama*, *A Shot of Ink*, and *Black Petals*.

Lonni was twice selected as a Writer in Residence at Hedgebrook, a writers retreat for women on Whidbey Island in Washington State. She's traveled to many countries and lived in several states and currently resides in Tucson, Arizona with her scientist husband, Jonathan and shows her art at a Tucson gallery. She's currently working on another novel.

"If I didn't know the Lees Sisters were chicks, I would think they were hard-drinking, gun-toting vigilantes from Brooklyn. Genius, pure genius, runs in the Lees gene pool."

Cindy Rosmus, Editor, *Yellow Mama*

www.ingramcontent.com/pod-product-compliance
Lightning Source LLC
Chambersburg PA
CBHW020319260626
47156CB00004B/1298

COLD BULLETS
AND HOT BABES

Detour if you dare into the dark alleys and twisted cul-de-sacs of the human heart. Brush shoulders with men whose eyes are as hard and cold as bullets—murderers, grifters, and hapless goofballs, who prey on the innocent and unsuspecting, often at their own peril.

Against your better judgment, get up close and intimate with sizzling kiss-and-kill babes, and live to tell about it...or not!

Eight hard-edged tales of criminals, killers, and their delectable molls.

Borgo Press Books by ARLETTE LEES

Cold Bullets and Hot Babes: Dark Crime Stories

COLD BULLETS AND HOT BABES

DARK CRIME STORIES

ARLETTE LEES

THE BORGO PRESS

MMXI

COLD BULLETS AND HOT BABES

FIRST EDITION

Published by Wildside Press LLC

www.wildsidebooks.com

DEDICATION

To The Memory of My Grandmother,

Mae E. Lees,

Who taught us the love of books;

And to

My teacher and friend,

Hannah Folsom,

Who said I'd write one.

CONTENTS

INTRODUCTION

When arrogant smart-ass Jeeter Tate ventures into Louisiana's BLOOD BAYOU, he finds more trouble than he bargained for in the steamy underaged Cajun girl, Suzette, and her wild, certifiable brother Pierre.

BRUISED introduces Joey McFeeny, a city cop on medical leave, and his brothers, Pug the gangster and Mick the parish priest. But, will they step over the line in seeking justice in the disappearance of their missing sister?

TROUBLE IN GUNNAR presents us with two brave youngsters trying to survive the powers of evil after their widowed father rushes into marriage with a strange woman with a mysterious past.

CASH is a seasoned grifter who preys on innocent and unsuspecting women like sweet golden-haired Carly and the darkly alluring Greta. But lounge lizard Cash might be in for a surprise or two.

Until beautiful Frances Bulger became pregnant and was expelled from parochial school, she had been known as Irish Rose in her blue collar neighborhood. After watching Frances grow fatter and more apathetic with each passing year, her daughter Rosemary, AGAINST ALL ODDS, is determined to go down a different road.

Our youthful protagonists in LAST CHANCE IN GUNNAR struggles to survive the abusive and neglectful parents who are supposed to be watching out for them. They fight, not only for their dignity as human beings, but against the dark shadow of

their past.

If you are a fan of classic pulp fiction, ANGEL DOLL was written for you. Jaded alcoholic ex-cop Jack Dunning and the delicate, sensuous, dime-a-dance girl, Angel, seek salvation in one another's embrace, willing to give love one last chance on the mean, Depression-era streeets of Little Ireland.

Our journey concludes with the poignant poem, FAMILY MYTHOLOGY, about a boy's devotion to his violent and emotionally complex Uncle Mick.

—Arlette Lees

ACKNOWLEDGMENTS

THESE STORIES WERE previously published as follows, and are reprinted (with minor editing, updating, and textual modifications) by permission of the author:

"Blood Bayou" was originally published in *Hardboiled* #41, January 2010, and also in *Whodunit?: The First Borgo Press Book of Crime and Mystery Stories*, edited by Robert Reginald, Borgo Press, 2011. Copyright © 2010, 2011 by Arlette Lees.

"Bruised" was originally published in *Hardboiled* #37, March 2008. Copyright © 2008, 2011 by Arlette Lees.

"Trouble in Gunnar" was originally published in *Deadly Dames*, Bold Venture Press, 2009. Copyright © 2009, 2011 by Arlette Lees.

"Cash" was originally published in *Hardboiled* #35, Spring 2006. Copyright © 2006, 2011 by Arlette Lees.

"Family Mythology" was originally published in *Hardboiled* #35, Spring 2006. Copyright © 2006, 2011 by Arlette Lees.

"Against All Odds," "Last Chance in Gunnar," and "Angel Doll" are published here for the first time. Copyright © 2011 by Arlette Lees.

BLOOD BAYOU

Jeeter Tate hit the ground running—well, he might as well have been running considering the condition of his old Ford pickup. With a burp and a backfire he headed out of Bakersfield in a cloud of dust, his radiator boiling over on the long stretches of desert between California and Texas.

Jeeter was born in Texas and so was Charleen. Her five burley brothers were still there, fighting dogs, selling white lightning, biting the heads off chickens to freak out neighbors who wandered too close to the property line. Jeet had no way of explaining Charleen's absence, so he limped the truck across the state line into Louisiana's alligator country.

God, how he wished he'd never hooked up with Charleen, but like all the other high school guys he'd salivated at the sight of her juicy little bod. She was the cutest girl on the cheerleading squad with her fluffy blonde curls and bouncy boobs.

She'd fallen for him too, like a ton of bricks, just like the other hot babes that ran their fingers through his jet black shag of hair and gazed into his paler than pale blue eyes. Charleen said they were the color of moonlight reflected through a Coke bottle. Now, how many dudes had eyes this color? One in a thousand? Hell no, Jeeter knew he was one in a million.

When he started dating Charleen his cousin Huey told him there was no way she could get knocked up if they did it standing up. That method of family planning failed right off the bat and Huey laughed his fool head off even after Jeeter blackened his eye.

Three years married and there were already two squalling rugrats on the scene. He hadn't known babies were capable of such heroic vocalization. He'd morphed from devil-may-care Romeo to a trained monkey on a short leash.

Charleen had managed to keep her trim figure and good looks while his were slipping faster than a clown on a banana peel, especially after he lost his two front teeth in a bar fight over a redheaded waitress. She might have had the decency to mention that her husband harbored unrealistic expectations regarding her fidelity.

"If you'd stay home where you belong these things wouldn't happen," said Charleen, rocking baby Skeezix in her arms. What a know-it-all! Next she'd be filing for divorce, asking for alimony and child support. First, she'd have to prove those brats were really his.

As if things weren't bad enough, he lost his job at the auto repair shop. He'd taken Mayor Stapleton's Lincoln for a joy ride when it came in for a lube. Except for the ding in the passenger side door and a rear flat tire, he'd returned it in pristine condition.

When Charleen took the last five bucks he'd earmarked for a pack of smokes and bought lotto tickets he'd had it. He broke into the repair shop after midnight and treated himself to some well-deserved severance pay. Even then, there was hardly enough cash to make it worth his while.

Almost out of money, he'd pulled into a clapboard grocery store on the edge of a mosquito-infested swamp. It wasn't where he'd intended to end up, but his map was in shreds and he'd lost the main road about an hour back. He thumped a bottle of Jack Daniel's and a bag of chitlins on the counter.

"Hey, Pierre," said the old witch behind the cash register. "I thought you never came off the bayou." What a ding-bat! "Looks like you had a rough night, mon."

He caught his reflection in the plastic donut case, a face thorny with stubble, hair as dirty as a mechanic's rag.

"Ya, one hell of a night," he said. The old crone looked like a

voodoo queen in her Mardi Gras beads and towering head wrap. He'd seen fewer wrinkles on mummies. He told her to take off her mask, that Halloween was over. She pointed an arthritic finger in his direction and mumbo-jumbo'd a death curse that made him roar with laughter as he walked out the door.

What a weird backwater dump!

As he walked to his truck a mail carrier pulled into the lot.

"Hey, Pierre!" he called, with a friendly wave. Jeeter looked behind him but no one was there. What the hell? Back in California they called strangers dude or bro and laid on a high five. In Texas it was bubba or cowboy delivered with a playful punch to the shoulder. Pierre had to be a Louisiana thing.

The carrier shoved a passel of mail in Jeeter's hand. "You've saved me a trip up Bayou Sang," he said. "Give my regards to old man Devereaux." He jumped back in his truck and was gone, leaving Jeeter standing there with his mouth open.

Bayou Sang? Jeeter got a D in French, but he was no dummy. He knew that *sang* meant blood. Blood Bayou?

He speculated on the contents of the envelopes. Some were addressed to Rémy Devereaux and a few to Pierre Marquet, Rt. 3, Bayou Sang. He could rip them open for the hell of it, check for cash, then scatter the letters along the roadside.

He'd been running on empty for about seven miles or so. He tapped the odometer but it had crapped out on him. He pulled into the first station he came to even though it looked like a throwback to the 1930s with its rusty pumps and a sign that hung from one hinge. The bony attendant shuffled out in baggy overalls, pumped his gas and cleaned the bugs off the windshield. He looked as if he'd blown in from the Dust Bowl.

"That'll be eighty bucks, Mr. Marquet."

Eighty fuckin' bucks! That brought him back to the twenty first century. After doling out the cash he only had ten bucks left from the heist. And there it was again, someone thinking he was this Pierre Marquet fellow.

He checked the map that was taped to the office window. The turn-off to Bayou Sang was only three miles up the road,

not a town really, but a large swampy district. The mail would be a perfect excuse to pay this guy a visit. He could case the joint while he was there, maybe come back in the night and rip something off.

The dirt track that cut through the swamp was almost impassable. Trees blocked the sun creating perpetual twilight. Jeeter clanked over potholes, dodged razor-sharp cypress knees and slid in places where the swamp had swallowed the road.

Eight maybe ten miles down the road and he hadn't seen one house, not even a shack, just an occasional pirogue gathering moss at the water's edge. Strange animal sounds emanated from the shadows. The engine light went on. Maybe this wasn't such a good idea after all, risking his tires, running out his gas. He was about to turn around when he came to a dented mailbox in front of a clearing. DEVERE had been slopped on the side with black paint before the artistic genius ran out of space.

He swung the truck into a large yard of swept dirt in front of an unpainted house of cypress boards. The back deck straddled the bayou on stilts and pecan and willow trees shaded the roof. He'd expected a third world hovel of some kind but this was actually pretty damn nice.

By the time he'd switched off the engine the truck was surrounded by a noisy pack of redbone hounds. A man at work in a tomato patch dropped his shovel and picked up a shotgun that was leaning against a shed. He strode over, his gnarled bare feet kicking up the dust. He gave the dogs a few casual kicks. They let out a yelp or two and crawled under the porch, disappointed at having missed the opportunity of tearing Jeeter limb from limb.

Jeeter opened the truck door, climbed out and extended his hand.

"I'm Jeeter Tate," he said.

The moment they touched hands a jolt of electricity zapped across the synapse between them. They were a mirror image of one another right down to the black hair and paler than pale blue eyes. The noses were the same, the cheekbones, the planes

of the forehead. The only difference Jeet could see was that the Cajun had managed to hang on to all of his teeth.

"*Mon dieu!*" said Pierre.

"Holy shit!" said Jeeter.

Pierre leaned into Jeeter's face like an entomologist examining a bug under glass, judging the stranger to be a strikingly handsome replica of himself.

Jeeter slapped his knee and laughed. "I guess everyone does have an identical twin," he said. "Looks like we've found ours."

"*Qui sont vous, mon ami?*" said Pierre.

"Sorry, *compadre*, I don't speak the lingo." He reached inside his jacket and handed Pierre the mail. "There's also some stuff here for a Mr. Devereaux."

"*Oui*, poor Uncle Rémy." The Cajun spoke English but it was obviously his second language. "He was visiting in New Orleans when Katrina hit. That was over a month ago and we haven't heard a word."

"Well, he's probably a goner," said Jeet.

Pierre yelled toward the house.

"Suzette, get out here."

The woman who pushed through the screen door held a fluffy white dog under her arm. She had a doe-eyed angel face, her long wavy hair was like soft black smoke. She did a double take when she saw Jeeter.

"My God, Pierre, he could be your identical twin!" Her English was far better than her brothers like maybe she'd had some schooling. Third grade. Maybe fourth.

"Jeeter Tate, ma'am." If he'd had a hat he would have tipped it. "Just call me Jeet," he said. Oh baby, call me anything, call me a dog and I'll lick your toes and work my way up.

"My sister," said Pierre. Jeeter was praying he wouldn't hear the 'wife' word.

Woo! Woo! Woo! Things were sure looking up for old Jeet.

He figured her age between fourteen and twenty. He was never very good when it came to guessing. Her simple cotton shift was sheer from too many washings and what didn't show

through the thin fabric was implied in the way it clung to every curve and crevice of her nubile body. She peeked at him through a lock of hair. Her look was sweet and smoldering.

Woo! Woo! Woo! thought Jeet. I've died and gone to heaven.

Pierre caught the intimate exchange and let out a full-throated whoop of laughter.

A couple hounds started scrabbling among the tomato plants. Pierre cursed in French and raised the shotgun.

"Don't shoot!" yelled Jeet without thinking. The gun went off with a deafening bang that left his ears ringing. The shot whizzed over the dog's heads as they bounded for the trees. Pierre laughed and gave him a good-natured slap on the back.

"Come, *mon ami*," he said. "We have plenty of chicken and dirty rice on the stove."

Jeeter would have eaten horse shit if it meant getting closer to Suzette. When they entered the house, Pierre set his shotgun inside the door. Jeeter wasn't quite sure what he thought of the guy but he felt a lot safer once the Cajun's finger was off the trigger.

They ate at a picnic table on the deck above the swamp. Free-range chickens picked at the cooked rice Suzette scattered on the boards. It was the first decent meal Jeeter had had in days. Afterward they relaxed in lounge chairs. Reeds and water lilies grew along the water's edge. If it weren't for the damn mosquitoes it would have been the Garden of Fuckin' Eden. He could sure get used to a life like this. Charleen and the boys already seemed like a mistake from another lifetime.

Jeeter caught Suzette's eye and moved his chair closer to hers. She lifted her knee and he watched her skirt flutter upward toward her hips. Her golden skin glowed in the ambient humidity and the pungent scent of arousal hung in the air. Pierre grew silent, smoked a dark cigarette that looked French or Turkish and looked on with a combination of wariness and amusement. Jeet wished he could read his mind but the French don't let you know what they're really thinking.

"What if your beau decided to drop in at this very moment?"

he asked.

"Sheriff DuBois?" said Suzette. Jeeter's stomach roiled. Sheriff's carried guns. He didn't like the sound of that. After all, meddling with another man's woman was how he lost his teeth. "Until he pops the question I'm free to do as I please." She smiled and looked at the stranger who wore her brother's face, his hair, his pale blue eyes. There was something dangerous about him, territory as yet unexplored. She felt the visceral pull of consanguinity, both forbidden and irresistible.

A pair of huge golden eyes broke the surface of the water at the edge of the deck and the spell was broken. Jeeter sat bolt upright.

"What the hell is that?"

Pierre looked at him as if he were from another planet.

"It's just an alligator," said Pierre. "Where you say you're from?"

"California," he said. As far as Pierre was concerned that was another planet.

"Just don't dangle your feet in the water," said Suzette. "They come for dinner scraps." She might have let him in on that bit of information a little sooner.

Pierre tossed a handful of chicken bones into the water. A few more prehistoric reptiles swam over, snapping and churning the surface. Jeeter wasn't half so relaxed anymore, a bit nauseous and weak in the knees. He walked to the truck and returned with the bottle of whiskey.

The moment he saw Suzette's face he knew he'd made a big mistake. She gave him a frightened look but Pierre was already headed into the house for glasses. Jeeter gave a helpless shrug. "I'm sorry," he mouthed. She looked like she was going to cry.

"He's crazier than a shithouse rat when he drinks," she said. "Just one drink and he starts beating the crap out of me. Without Uncle Rémy here to protect me...." She let the thought hang. "You'd better hit the road before he starts in."

When Pierre returned with the glasses the white dog began to tremble. "It's all right, Bon-Bon," she said, stroking his fur.

Jeeter decided he'd seen enough of Bayou Sang, but how could he make a diplomatic exit without joining Pierre in at least one shot?

Before long Pierre had foregone the civility of glasses and drank straight from the bottle. First Jeet had run out half his gas getting here, now the Cajun was swilling down the last of his booze, stomping his feet, singing Jolie Blonde in French, the deck vibrating like a trampoline. The more he thundered on the boards the more alligators crashed the party.

Pierre reached down and grabbed a red hen that was picking at grains on rice. He started swinging her by the neck.

"Ain't this the old biddy don't lay eggs no more?" he said.

Suzette rose on shaky legs and set Bon-Bon on the deck.

"Give her to me, Pierre. She's a pet. Stop acting crazy."

"Crazy like this?" he said, tossing the hen in a high flapping arch over the water. The biggest gator almost stood on his tail as he broke the surface. He caught the bird with a snap of mighty jaws, threw his head back a few times and swallowed the bird whole. The color drained from Jeeter's face.

"Well, it's getting a little late for me," he said, rising.

"What, I make you nervous, *garçon*?" said Pierre.

The Cajun reached out and grabbed Suzette by the arm.

"Stop playing around," she said. Her voice trembled. She suddenly looked about ten years old and very small.

He dragged her toward the edge of the deck and she screamed. Bon-Bon growled. He sounded as ferocious as a squeaky-toy. He did however manage to sink his small sharp teeth into Pierre's big toe. He cursed, released his sister and snatched the dog up by the collar. Jeeter could no longer distinguish the dog's high-pitched yips from the girl's shrieks. A flood of adrenaline coursed through his veins and his nerves snapped like fiddle strings. He drove a hard-soled shoe into Pierre's groin and Pierre dropped the dog to the deck. Shit! Why had he done that? The Cajun would kill him if he was ever able to stand up straight again. From his hunkered down position Pierre looked sideways with a dangerous fire in his blue eyes. He reached out with a

massive hand and grabbed the cuff of Jeeter's jeans.

Jeeter freaked and jerked loose with such ferocity that the sudden release of tension sent the Cajun stumbling backward toward the edge of the deck. Jeeter instinctively reached out to pull him back to safety but it was too late. Pierre plummeted downward with a splash. His scream sounded like the roar of a chain saw, its echo reverberating through the swamp.

Bon-Bon flew into the house and Jeeter and Suzette looked down into the churning water. The king gator had his jaws clamped around Pierre's torso. He death-rolled, thrashing and spinning until the water boiled with blood. The gator sank beneath the surface with Pierre in his deadly grip. For Jeeter it was surreal, like watching himself being eaten alive.

As suddenly as it had begun it was over. A snowy egret flapped into the branches of a cypress tree, the orange ball of sun sank low on the horizon, bream jumped among the lily pads and the gators were gone.

"I'm outta here," said Jeeter. "That's about all the excitement I can take for one day. Your brother got drunk and fell in. End of story."

Suzette was shaking. She threw her arms around his waist. It was at least eighty degrees out but her body had turned cold with shock.

"Don't go," she said. "Not yet. I've never been alone out here at night. What if Pierre comes crawling out of the swamp?"

Jeeter's eyes bugged. "Believe me, that ain't going to happen."

She rested her head on his chest and he felt her soft-as-smoke hair against his cheek. He should really run like hell, as far from Bayou Sang as he could get, but her body began to warm to his embrace and he could feel her breasts burning through the thin cotton of his Harley-Davidson t-shirt. She smelled of fear and sex and French perfume. He was a goner.

"You can leave in the morning," she said. "but tonight I need someone to take care of me." She looked as young and defenseless as an orphan fawn, so young in fact that he didn't want to nail her down on specifics.

The crickets were in full chorus and a silver moon was rising above the cypress swamp. She took him by the hand and led him to the bedroom. "It's all right," she said. "I need for you to hold me."

He did a lot more than hold her and their love-making proved an anesthetic against the terrors of the afternoon. She was by turns a kitten and a tiger, passive and submissive, gentle and fierce. She gave him everything he so desperately desired, indulged his every fantasy and even a few he hadn't thunk up yet. Oh yes, this little cookie had been down the same road before, probably with the Sheriff who wanted the milk but wasn't quite ready to buy the cow.

Then he told her his story...at least the story he thought she might like to hear, about how his beloved wife had died in an auto accident before they'd had a chance to create the family they'd so desperately dreamed of...well, that's how he wished it had happened.

Deep into the night she whispered in his ear. "You can stay if you want to." He'd told her how he was wandering the world alone and lost, almost giving up hope of ever being loved again. She'd swallowed it hook, line and sinker. "You can stay and become Pierre."

"What do you mean?"

"You look like his identical twin. You could pull it off. You could play the part when people are around and when we're alone it can be just like this," and she kissed him with her warm, moist lips. "There would never be any questions about what happened this afternoon. We didn't do anything wrong, but it could get complicated."

He mulled that over for a moment. Having the run of the place was a hell-of-a-lot better than ripping it off for a few toma-toes out of the garden and some old fishing tackle. And since the silky, young Suzette was part of the deal...well, what hot-blooded, testosterone-fueled male wouldn't go for that?

"Sounds good to me," said Jeeter.

Jeeter slept late and woke alone in the big bed. When he got

up to take a piss he noticed that Suzette must have driven his truck into town. He got dressed and didn't think much about it until she came into the yard from the road on foot. He walked out onto the porch. The redbones sniffed at him but soon became bored and wandered off.

"Where's my truck?" he said.

"Gone. I sank it in the bayou a few miles from here. You can't afford to be connected with it."

"WHAT?" He felt trapped like he wasn't getting enough oxygen. Other than his truck, he didn't have a pot to pee in.

"Don't get so excited. You can drive Pierre's truck. Besides, if you ever blow your cover things could get sticky very fast. It's always the stranger passing through that takes the fall for anything that goes bad on the bayou."

Put that way, it made sense. Besides, the old Ford was crapping out and he was tired of fixing it.

He heard the distant growl of an engine. It sounded like a high-powered car and it was coming closer.

"Quick," said Suzette. "This is your big test. Put on a pair of Pierre's overalls and get rid of those citified shoes."

A sheriff's car swept into the yard amid a cyclone of dust. Jeet peeked around the bedroom curtain. A tall bull mastiff of a man unfolded his bulk and slammed the car door behind him. The redbones rubbed against his legs like he was the leader of the pack. Good-lookin' guy, all teeth and smiles like a young Burt Lancaster. Jeet tried to calm his nerves. There was no way the word of his heist could have made its way to the Louisiana bayou. He found a pair of overalls and climbed into them.

"Étienne," said Suzette. "What brings you off the beaten track?" She threw her arms around his neck and he swung her in a circle with casual intimacy. Jeeter's blood boiled. Étienne set her back on the ground.

"I wish I had better news," he said, "but, Rémy's friends in New Orleans have no idea where he is. They fear the worst."

"What now?" she asked.

"Just wait and pray, I guess." He cupped her breasts in his big

paws. "You still have those handcuffs I gave you? You still want to be my little Prisoner of Zenda?" She giggled.

Enough of this shit. Jeeter gathered his courage and stepped outside. The lovebirds drifted apart.

"Any word from Uncle Rémy?" he asked. He lacked Pierre's tough calluses and the stones beneath his tender feet hurt like hell.

"Nothing to hang your hopes on," said the sheriff. DuBois looked him up and down. Jeet's mouth went dry. "You lose weight, Pierre?"

"I've had the flu or something. Lost my appetite." If DuBois noticed the sudden loss of the two front teeth he didn't say anything. Lack of teeth was almost a residency requirement back in the boonies.

After he drove away Jeet was light-headed with relief. Suzette laughed and threw her arms around his neck. "If you can fool Étienne, you can fool anyone."

"You two an item or what?" He was jealous when it came to his women, but that didn't mean he wouldn't set aside his moral compass if it got in the way of a hot one night stand.

"Not anymore," she said.

"Since when?"

"Since last night, *Monsieur.*" She kissed him and probed between his lips with her tongue. He thought he'd explode before they made it to the bed.

Suzette had one evening dress, a red, strapless chiffon that fell just above the knee. After dark Jeeter dressed like a local yokel and they headed to a juke joint back in the woods so he could get a feel for Cajun culture.

The juke was a plain, square building that sat on pier blocks in a grove of willow and pecan trees. The wood floor was strewn with sawdust, cigarette butts and spilled beer. Everyone from toddlers to octogenarians stomped and hooted to Doug Kershaw's rendition of Jambalaya. Jeeter sized up the crowd... clannish as gypsies...fiercely self-sufficient...incurably fun-loving. But, beneath the gaiety he could smell feral undertones.

Scratch a dog you get a wolf. Scratch a Cajun and you're in deep shit. Pierre was proof of that.

The energy in the room was dizzying until the bartender jerked the juke box cord out of the wall and the music stopped. A roar of protest went up from the crowd.

The bartender turned up the small TV that sat on the end of the bar. "I want to hear this," he said. "Somebody in California won that big lotto."

"Who gives a shit?" yelled a joker who could barely stand on his own two feet. Everybody laughed.

"Let's watch," said Suzette, dragging him over to the bar.

"Tonight, ladies and gentlemen, we have a true Cinderella story," said the announcer. A state lottery representative handed a pretty blonde lady one of those over-sized checks for 5.3 million dollars. Jeeter's jaw hit the floor. "Mrs. Jeeter Tate of Bakersfield has been working three jobs to support her two darling little boys since being abandoned by her husband who robbed his former place of employment and vanished." The announcer looked straight into Jeeter's eyes through the TV. "How are things hanging with you Mr. Tate? Mrs. Tate just hired a big Hollywood divorce lawyer."

Charleen was the golden girl of the moment. She was smiling and gracious and the camera loved her. Jeeter was devastated. He'd hoped his sudden departure would throw her into a state of catatonic despair and now she looked twice as good as she had before he dumped her.

He was shocked at the injustice of it all. She'd bought those lotto tickets with *his* five bucks. The winnings should be half his. By rights, it should be *all* his. What did she ever do to earn it except cook, clean, do laundry, take care of the kids, mow the lawn, wash the cars...? He'd completely forgotten about Suzette. He had to get back to California and make a case for himself. He turned on the bar stool in time to see her heading out the door in a huff. Trouble in paradise.

"Wait, sweet thing. I can explain."

Her hands were frozen on the steering wheel as they drove

back to the house. She looked straight ahead. When they pulled to a stop she ran through the front door. Jeeter grabbed her arm and she pulled free.

"Your beloved wife seems to have risen from her grave," she said.

"Just listen to me for a second."

"Cajun men do not abandon their families no matter how hard things get. I want you to take your things and go."

"Listen baby, those winnings are half mine. All I have to do is get to California to stake my claim. When I come back with all that dough we'll be rich. We'll live like kings."

"The way I live right now suits me fine." Her voice was steady, her eyes as cold and hard as concrete. "I'm asking you to leave my house."

"Okay," he said. "Just give me the keys to the truck."

"You don't have a truck." He felt that one coming.

"BECAUSE YOU SANK IT!" Blood rushed to his head and roared in his ears.

"If you hadn't overreacted Pierre would still be alive and you wouldn't be in this fix. I warned you. I told you to leave before he started acting crazy."

Bon-Bon looked at Suzette with worried eyes. He whined softly.

Jeeter grabbed her purse and fished out the keys to the truck. He saw the handcuffs in the bottom of the bag. They struggled briefly until he heard her finger snap and she let go with a cry of pain. She took off a high heeled shoe and went for his face. The stiletto caught the corner of his eye. It teared up and clamped shut. He let out an angry bellow.

He grabbed her by the hair, dragged her into the bedroom and threw her unceremoniously on the bed. To think that just last night things were going so well. Bon-Bon started yapping and running in circles on the bedspread.

"All right," she said. "Take the truck and go. Just go."

His knee was planted in the center of her chest. He twisted her arm and cuffed it to the iron headboard.

"Étienne is going to kill you," she said, her soft black hair falling over one eye.

"Thanks to you baby, he doesn't know I exist."

The redbones alerted to the row. They were growling deep in their throats. Their toenails clicked as they paced back and forth on the porch. And there was something else. A more subtle sound. He stopped and listened. It stopped. It had been a soft thumping, a tap, tap, tap, the kind of noise a boat makes when it knocks against the dock.

Suzette's chest rose and fell beneath his weight. Her breasts strained against the delicate fabric of her dress. The frightened fawn look was back but now it angered him. He ripped the bodice of her dress down to the waist. Let her go juking in that, he thought spitefully. He stopped breathing. There it was again, coming from the direction of the deck. Tap. Tap. Tap. Every time he concentrated on it, it stopped.

He reached out to touch the girl's bare breast. The dog nailed him good, bit his thumb to the bone. That little son-of-a-bitch. He threw a lamp but by the time it hit the wall the dog was far under the bed.

Women! They were the cause of all his problems. Any fool could see that. First Charleen goes and gets knocked up. That was damn inconsiderate. Then Suzette sinks his truck and tells him to hit the road with only the clothes on his back. He slapped her a couple times in the face before he left the room...not so hard as he'd hit a man...I mean, he wasn't a monster...just enough to punish her for all the trouble she'd caused.

He rummaged through her purse and cleaned out her wallet. He heard something again. Suzette sobbed quietly from the bedroom but that wasn't it. He walked slowly to the back of the house and turned on the deck lights. Nobody out there. No raccoons wandering about. He stepped outside. Frogs croaked in the darkness beyond the circle of light. He slapped a mosquito on his neck. There was an occasional splash as fish jumped among the reeds.

He walked to the edge of the deck and looked down. For

some inexplicable reason he thought of the voodoo woman and her curse. You'd have to be a real hayseed to believe in that superstitious crap. Then again, he had to admit his nerves were a bit on edge.

Tap. Tap. Tap. He laughed out loud. There was a kid's white ball floating among the pilings. He shrugged off the tension. Then the ball rolled over and it didn't look so much like a ball anymore. The skulls mouth was open wide as if it wanted to go on screaming until Louisiana seceded from the union. One pale ice blue eye remained lodged in the socket. It stared right into Jeeter's face.

Jeet screamed all the way to the truck. He'd run the gamut of redbones, losing a pant leg and both of his shoes and sustaining various abrasions and contusions.

The moment Suzette heard the truck rip out of the yard she strained against the handcuff and with her free hand grabbed the cordless phone she kept under the edge of the bed. She punched in the number of the sheriff's department and broke into sobs when DuBois picked up.

Étienne flew over the wrecked road to Bayou Sang. His deputies intercepted Jeeter just before he turned onto the interstate. They hauled him into the station kicking and screaming and babbling about voodoo curses and a skull with a blue eye afloat in Blood Bayou.

"Pierre never was quite right in the head," said Deputy LaRoque.

"The booze finally fried his brain," said Deputy Chevalier.

Étienne found Suzette bruised, battered, and half-naked. The dog was curled up next to her shoulder. He wagged his tail when he saw the sheriff. The scene was self-explanatory, implying something vicious and incestuous. The sweet Suzette did nothing to correct the misconception. He released her from the cuff, took her in his arms and held her close to his chest.

"Pierre's gone crazy as a coon," she whispered.

"He's always been crazy as a coon. Don't you think it's time we tied the knot so I can take care of you?"

The prisoner swore up and down that he was not Pierre Marquet. He was Jeeter Tate and his wife just won the California lotto. He'd never eaten a crawdad in his life. He didn't speak French. He said he'd driven to Louisiana in a truck he couldn't locate and had identity papers he could not find. The deputies laughed their asses off.

Suzette was brought into the station to give a statement. "I've been living in terror for over a month," she said. "One night Pierre got drunk and attacked me. When Uncle Rémy came to my defense there was a terrible fight. Rémy knocked out two of Pierre's teeth...just look for yourself...at that point Pierre grabbed his shotgun and killed my uncle. He threw his body to the alligators. When I threatened to tell Étienne what had happened, he went nuts. He can make up any name he wants, but what other man has eyes like his?"

The D.A. heard every word from his chair in the corner.

"As absurd as it seems, let's give this man every opportunity to clear his name before he gets what's coming to him. Fly that woman out from California and we'll listen to what she has to say."

Jeeter breathed a sigh of relief. Suzette shifted nervously in her chair.

Charleen Tate walked into the interrogation room two days later. She looked like a million bucks in her pink Chanel suit and triple strand of pearls. Awaiting her arrival were Sheriff DuBois, Suzette, the D.A. and Jeeter.

"Baby doll," said Jeeter when she looked his way. "I'm so glad you came to clear things up."

"Well," said Étienne, "is this your husband?"

"I've never seen this man before in my life," she said.

"CHARLEEN! It's me, Jeeter, the father of those sweet baby boys."

Everyone in the room burst out laughing.

"Believe me, Sheriff," she said. "when you win the lotto

every Tom, Dick and Harry crawls out of the woodwork."

The D.A. extended his hand. "So sorry to have inconvenienced you Mrs. Tate. I think we now have all the evidence we need."

As she left the room she looked at Suzette and winked.

Out on Blood Bayou the moon turned the water to silver. Two skulls floated side by side downstream.

BRUISED

The digital clock read 3 A.M. when the phone jangled me out of my drug-induced sleep. Reaching for the receiver, I cursed, as I banged my bad knee on the nightstand. Mom's brogue was as thick as potato soup in my ear.

"It's Rory," she said, softly rolling her R's.

At the mention of my diminutive twenty-one-year-old sister, with her flying red hair and wild lifestyle, the pain in my shattered knee went into over drive. What now? A drunk and disorderly? Another DUI?

"Do we have to do this right now?" I croaked, through a haze of painkillers.

"She's missing, Joey. And she's pregnant."

I squinted as I snapped on the bedside lamp and threw a T-shirt over the shade.

"I know. They're talking about it in every bar on the strip. I wish she'd hooked up with some blue collar guy from the neighborhood, but no, it has to be some rich dandy in silk skivvies."

"And a coward to boot, slappin' her around so she can't even hide the bruises."

"Listen Mom, you think Stafford needs his ticket punched, call Pug. He's the muscle in the family."

I tapped a Camel out of the pack and lit it.

"Jesus, Mary and Joseph, you're the cop, Joey!"

"Remember my knee, Mom? The shotgun blast? The doc says I'm off that leg for six more weeks or I could lose it."

"That would never have stopped your Da when he was on

The Force. Listen, me boyo, Stafford is facing eighteen years of a rich man's child support. He told Rory he'd have her down at the clinic if he had to drag her by the hair."

Seemed reasonable to me, drugged up as I was.

"She's a good Catholic lass, Joey." I rolled my eyes. "This morning she went to have it out with Mr. Moneybags. No way that sweet girl could take care of her problem on Friday and face Mick at Sunday morning mass. Stafford says she never showed up at his place. He must think us MeFeeney's were born yesterday."

"I suppose you called the clinic."

"I'm way ahead of you there. They never heard of her. Worse yet, she hasn't shown up at The Emerald Isle all night."

Not showing up at her favorite haunt gave me pause.

"I'm thinkin' he really did her in this time," said Mom. "Stories about this guy go back to when your Da was walking the beat."

I rubbed my temples as the tumblers fell into place with an ominous click.

"Go back to bed, Mom. I'll look into it."

I punched out my smoke and burned my thumb. The ashtray tumbled upside down onto the rug. It was going to be one of those nights.

* * * * * * *

Like a 1930s movie star, Colby Stafford lounged in the doorway of his upscale townhouse in a burgundy satin robe, a teenage blonde with a black eye draped like a wilted daffodil over his arm.

Colby was fifty-ish, clean-shaven and cologned. If you looked closely, you could see sins crawling beneath his skin like tropical parasites.

"Oh God," he said, in a tone of casual dismissal. "Looks like Fannon McFeeney has sent the cavalry to look for little sister."

He lit a lavender cigarette with a gold-tipped filter. The girl

hovered over his shoulder. With a twitch of annoyance, he shrugged her away and she vanished with a pout.

"You got lucky tonight," I said. "Mom was ready to take Dad's service revolver and blow your prissy shit to kingdom come."

"You get the same answer I gave her. I haven't seen Rory in days."

I glimpsed past him into the foyer. He didn't stop me as I leaned heavily on my cane and limped past him. I grabbed a red purse off the entry table. Back on the stoop, I rummaged through the contents. It was full of Rory's personal items...driver's license...makeup...hair brush.

"Let's start over," I said.

Stafford gave a world-weary sigh and flicked the rest of his cigarette into the shrubbery.

"I lied. So fucking what? Rory kneed me in the groin when she found little Miss Tiffany in my bed. She left in a manic frenzy. That was about 10 P.M. That sister of yours is a poster child for ADD. She either needs to be medicated or zapped with a tranquilizer gun. Enough of her crap. I'm moving on with my life."

"Now that you've got her in a family way? How noble of you."

"Who says it was me knocked her up? It could be one of a dozen others for all I know."

I couldn't say if he was right or wrong, I just wanted to bust his face.

"DNA will clear that up fast enough," I said.

I handed him my card. He examined both sides with carefully manicured fingertips.

"I see you finally made Lieutenant. I'm impressed."

"Give me a call if your memory improves."

As he slipped the card into the pocket of his robe, I saw a fresh abrasion on his knuckles, the kind you get when you punch someone in the mouth and catch an incisor for your trouble.

"Mind if I go in and have a quick look around?"

"Got a warrant? If you're on active duty, I'm Peter Pan."

"Got something to hide?"

"Nothing that would interest you."

"How did you cut your hand?"

The skin tightened across his cheekbones and he blinked.

"That little mick?" he said, holding out his hand. "Tiffany had the audacity to contradict me, but she's young enough to learn."

"My sister was born talking back. She'll never learn."

We locked eyes. This time he didn't blink.

"Just one last question and I'll be out of your hair," I said. "When Rory left here, was it on her own steam or feet first?"

I landed on my bad knee at the bottom of the stairs before I realized I'd been socked in the jaw. A howl ripped from my throat. My cane rolled into the grass. The door slammed behind me and the porch light went out.

I'd underestimated the enemy. He was not only quick, he packed an iron punch. In Dad's day, I could have kicked in the damn door and shot him where he stood. Today you look cross-eyed at some murderous perp, you're dragged in front of Internal Affairs.

Officially, I was home on medical leave. I'd never been here. That didn't mean Stafford wouldn't pay for this. It just wouldn't be tonight. I pulled myself to my feet with a loud groan and pulled my cane out of the grass.

A neighbor stuck his head out of a second story window.

"Shut the fuck up or I'm calling the cops! People are trying to sleep here."

A cold rain fell as I drove down the strip. The bars were closed and the Rescue Mission was locked down for the night, its gold neon cross reflecting on the wet asphalt. There was no sign of Rory or her car, just a bum sleeping in the doorway of the pawn shop and a stray dog raiding a garbage can along the curb. My knee had ballooned to surreal proportions. The damp cold crept into my bones and I shuddered.

I collapsed in my easy chair with a brandy. Stafford had

made an effort to wipe blood from Rory's purse, but there was enough in the creases to warm the cockles of a lab tech's heart.

But, was it her blood? It could have been Tiffany's or even Stafford's. I was contemplating my next move when Pug called.

"Mom's been driving me nuts," he said.

"Tell me about it."

"One of Vin's boys found Rory's car by the old slaughterhouse. It had a flat. There was blood on the steering wheel and a cell phone in the mud. They checked the abandoned building but came up empty."

"Pug, Rory didn't own a cell phone. Did you hit redial?"

"The battery's dead." He cracked his knuckles, same as when we were kids and he was up tight. "I brought Mom up to date. She expects the worst, but doesn't she always. Who knows, this time she could be right." I heard him take a pull on his cigarette and cough the smoke out. "God forgive me, but dealing with Rory is like trying to take a shit in an outhouse full of bees. You can't get no peace."

I smiled.

"You're a real poet, Pug. I ever tell you that?"

I told him about my encounter with Stafford...the purse...the blood...the torn knuckles...the teen he was boinking. I sensed Pug's wheels turning in the silence.

"Meet me at The Aces," he said. "We'll put two and two together."

Pug, my younger brother, owns The Aces High Pub, a front for his gambling operation and other stuff I don't want to know about. Mick, my older brother, is a parish priest at St. Finnbar's. Me? I followed Dad into The Job after he took a bullet in the back a week before his retirement. That's us, just a typical family in Little Ireland, east of the factories.

* * * * * * *

I was in agony. I was out of pain pills and my knee was so

swollen it refused to bend. As dawn broke with a rumble of thunder, I dragged into Dr.'s On Duty on my way across town.

An M.D., who looked like a high school student, drained a liter of suspicious green fluid off the joint with a needle the size of a garden hose. He gave me an ominous look, like in the movies when the doc is about to saw your leg off.

He walked to the phone.

"Who's your doctor of record?"

"Look Doc, all I need is more pain pills."

"Not from me," he said. "You're staying off that leg, right?"

"Absolutely."

* * * * * * *

Vinnie Natoli was sitting at a table with Pug. He hadn't missed many meals since I'd seen him last. He had deep circles under his eyes and a few buttons missing from his vest.

"Well, if it ain't Quasimodo," he said, squinting through a toxic layer of cigar smoke. I hobbled across the room and eased painfully into a chair.

"We heard about the punk nailed you with the shotgun. Heard he was only seventeen."

"His first caper didn't go well. Until Father Nolan straightened out my shit, I was headed down the same dead end," I said.

I leaned my cane against the edge of the table and stretched my leg out in front of me. Vin looked at me and waved his cigar.

"Don't give me that shit," he said. "You never would have iced the clerk at the Likkor Lokker. He got what he had coming to him."

"It wasn't me," I said. "I was kissing the asphalt in the parking lot. My partner dropped him with a single shot through the left eye. Came out the back of his head, clean as a whistle."

"You mean Deborah Moskawitz saved your sorry ass?"

"That's the one."

"She used to beat me up and steal my lunch in fifth grade. Turned me on."

As Pug poured a round of eye-openers, I pulled Rory's purse and the cell phone from inside my raincoat and set them on the table. Rain hammered the roof above our heads and a tree of lightning bloomed on the horizon.

"Vin's got a dog in this fight too," said Pug.

Vin downed his shot. He sat quietly flexing the muscles in his jaw.

"How so?" I said, detecting the shift in mood.

"I had a cousin," said Vin. "Angie Milano. Guess who she was involved with when she vanished off the face of the earth?"

"Colby Stafford." I lit a smoke and leaned forward. "Tell me about it."

"Angie and Stafford got into it over something. I never knew what. He hit her in the head so hard she went deaf in one ear. The day she threatened to file a complaint she disappeared. She was only sixteen years old for crissake." He swallowed hard to loosen the tightness in his throat.

"She'll always be sixteen, if you know what I mean. That was seven years ago before you came on The Job. We never recovered so much as a tooth." His eyes were sad and dark as Italian olives. "She ain't the only girl dropped down the same black hole. You find so much as your sister's fingernail, you'll be the first who finds anything."

"I ran his name when Rory started seeing him. How come he comes up clean?"

"He's one of Supervisor Wright's most loyal contributors. Wright makes sure that the missing girls go down as runaways. Stafford knows to pick them young and wild, so when they ain't around no more, no one digs too deep. Angie gets buried in the cold case file with all them other missing girls."

Pug cracked his knuckles and lit a cigarette from the cinder of the one before it. We sat silently for a beat or two, rain ticking against the window.

"We don't close him down," said Pug, "no one else will."

Even if I trusted the veracity of Vin's account, I was apprehensive at being sucked into the dark vortex of his reality. I

wanted to think that I was removed...if only by a hair's breadth... from the world of thugs, gamblers and Italian gumbas with 'connections.'

I rubbed my tired eyes and shifted my knee to one more uncomfortable position.

"Let's slow down a minute," I said. "This is serious shit we're talking here. No need to go off half cocked."

"Slow down while he runs off to the Bahamas like he done when Angie went missing?"

I took an inventory of what we had...the pregnancy...the blood...Vin's cousin...my sister...Stafford's political connections with a less than sterling public figure. Then I asked myself if the world would be better or worse off if Stafford wasn't in it.

"Stafford's tough, or he wouldn't still be around. He'll have his guard up," I said.

Vin hunched forward, conspiratorially.

"Just hear me out," he said. "Every Saturday night at nine sharp, my nephew Gino picks Stafford up at the townhouse and drives him across the river to the Carnival Club. Let's say tonight we put the limo at your disposal. Do whatcha gotta do, just don't leave no evidence behind. Gino's working his way through college and don't need no complications in his life, like blood, hair, that kind of shit."

I downed my shot and took a Trappist moment to clear my head. Vin thumped back in his chair and threw his hands in the air.

"Stop worrying for crissake! It'll be dark and stormy. He'll never see it coming."

"Okay," I said. "Tonight."

Pug poured a second round of shots. I tossed mine back and felt it warm the edges of my healing ulcer.

Vin grew pensive.

"I can't believe Rory's gone," he said. "She was the life of the party in our senior year at Finney. The nuns never knew what to make of her. I used to follow her around like a puppy dog. I wonder why she never gave me a tumble."

Pug butted out his cigarette and shook his head.

"Listen Vin, the kid had lousy taste in men. You were too good a guy to make her list of losers."

After a few more shots, Vin rolled out the door into the rain. When he pulled away from the curb in his 1948 pink Caddy, he had a smile wrapped around his fat cigar.

Pug walked over and set an ashtray on the pool table where a leak had broken through.

"We're going to have our hands full with Stafford," he said. "We're going to need Mick behind the wheel."

I slowly stubbed out my smoke and limped over to where he was standing.

"I hate to get a priest mixed up in this," I said.

Pug rested his elbows on the pool table, his blue eyes burning with intensity.

"So, we should use Vin and he calls in the favor up the road? You really want to get in that deep with the gumbas?"

"You have a point. I guess we clean up our own side of the street."

I made it to the phone behind the bar. The fluid was building up on my knee again and I felt slightly disoriented. I punched in Mick's number and his housekeeper, Mrs. Healy, answered. I heard her slippers pad away from the phone.

"Father McFeeney," she called. "It's trouble on the phone."

He moaned sleepily.

"Pug or Joey?" he asked.

* * * * * * *

By the time night fell, the streets were rushing with water. Shingles were blown from rooftops and broken branches littered the roadways. Mick looked the part of a proper limo driver in his priestly casuals and Gino's shiny brimmed cap.

Mick's nose was as flat as a boxer's from all the scrapes he'd been in growing up on the streets of Little Ireland, and his beefy face was as knuckly as his fists. There wasn't a wife-beater or

gang-banger he hadn't dumped on his ass.

Mick let me and Pug off a block up from Stafford's townhouse, then circled back to make the pickup. I felt like a wreck, stumbling around on my cane, but without it I couldn't even stand. My face burned with fever and I felt a vague disconnect with my surroundings, like I was walking in someone else's dream.

Pug peered down the block and watched the roof light go on in the limo.

"The bastard fell for it," he said.

My face was so hot that rain steamed off of my skin. Water streamed from the visors of our caps.

"Here they come," said Pug.

Mick splashed the limo to the curb, filling our shoes with water. I walked around the car, opened the back seat driver's side door, plopped down on the seat and punched my revolver into Stafford's ribs.

Pug opened the opposite door and there sat the blonde, looking as hot as a pistol in a short sequined mini and blue fox jacket.

Mick shot me a chastising look in the rear view.

Okay, okay, so that small detail fell off my radar.

Pug was fast on his feet, didn't miss a beat. He reached into his wallet, pressed a crisp fifty in her hand and left her sputtering on the street corner outside Kelly's Bar, rain dripping into her silver shoes.

"Just what we need," said Mick. "A fuckin' witness to a kidnapping. That'll be five Our Father's and three Hail Mary's."

"What the fuck!" said Stafford, looking first at me, then at Mick. "Where the hell is Gino?"

"Just relax," said Pug, his voice husky from smoking.

"Hey, wait a minute. If this is about Rory, I already told you...."

"We can make it about her," I said, "or let's see, we can make it about Angie Milano."

Bull's-eye.

Stafford turned a sallow shade of corpse gray. I knew then that everything Vin had told us was right on the button.

"I didn't think you micks hung with the wops," he said. "They're always talking shit, probably have it on their morning cereal. Besides, no body, no crime. Go ahead and arrest me. My Jew lawyer will have me out in an hour."

Mick tossed his clerical collar on the seat beside him.

"He thinks we're bringing him to the station," he said, with a grin.

The three of us burst into laughter, like when we were kids and up to no good. .

"No body, no crime," said Pug, and we laughed and laughed.

We drove beyond the city lights to a marsh along the river where an abandoned fish cannery rotted on the bank.

Stafford walked quietly now, caged in by three Irish mesomorphs with murder on their minds. I was trembling with fever, my cane barely able to support my sagging weight.

"You okay?" asked Pug.

"Sure," I said.

"No you're not," he said, and removed the gun from my unsteady hand.

The floorboards of the old cannery were mushy beneath our feet, the bones of the building full of termites and rot. I shone my flashlight into a watery abyss where a section of floor had fallen twenty or thirty feet into the river below.

"Let's get the job done and get the hell out of here," I said.

Mick turned to Stafford.

"For the sake of your eternal soul, clear your conscience and tell us where the girl's remains are buried so I can give you final absolution."

"You unmitigated hypocrite!" screeched Stafford, a tear in the corner of one eye.

The building shook in the wind and my eyes wandered back to the hole in the floor. Quick as a rattler, Stafford's hard-soled shoe sank into the soft swollen pulp of my bad knee.

I shrieked like a demented banshee and my flashlight tumbled

end over end into the churning water below. Then, with a startling crunch that sounded like the breaking of giant bones, a section of floor gave way and Stafford plummeted downward into the abyss.

Mick's jaw dropped.

"Holy Mother of God!" he said.

The river had swallowed Stafford in a single gulp. No sound or movement came from the bottom of the pit. Not a scream. Not a cry. Just the swirling of the black water and the sound of rain clicking on the roof.

Pug pocketed my piece and sputtered a laugh.

"Wasn't us done it," he said. "We're outta here."

"Help me," I said. "He got me a good one."

With a brother on each arm I was dragged none too tenderly to the limo. I was unaware of my agonal moaning until Mick said, "Shake it off! What would Da say if he saw you whimpering like a little girl?"

* * * * * * *

Later that night in the E.R., Dr. Mercer chewed my ass out as he drained my knee and wrapped it.

"Don't bother telling me how it happened," he said. "I'm surprised any of you McFeeney boys made it to adulthood."

He snatched up my chart and walked out of the exam room.

"Doc, what about my pain pills?" I called after him.

* * * * * * *

The next morning I lay in bed with a knee that looked like a purple watermelon. When I heard the front door hit the inside wall, I hoped someone had come to shoot me and put me out of my misery. My heart jolted in my chest when Rory flew into the bedroom, her green eyes flashing, her lip decorated with stitches.

"Well, and if it isn't you malingerin' when you ought to be

confessing your sins at Sunday Mass," she said. "I know you have my purse and you'd better not have been snooping through it."

"We thought you were dead!" I exploded. "Mom's out of her mind with the worry of it all."

"Come on, Joey. Give me a break. The old battle axe does it to herself. If she wasn't busy poking into our private lives, she wouldn't know what to do with herself. Leave it to her to make all those embarrassing inquiries as to my whereabouts." She put her hands on her hips. "It doesn't look like you were all that worried, makin' the most of your wee injury."

My blood pressure shot up and the pain in my knee went into overdrive.

"Where the hell have you been and what have you done to your face?"

She suddenly ran out of steam and sat on the corner of the bed with a dramatic sigh.

"I finally got up the nerve to face Colby. We fought. He punched me in the mouth. So, what's new there? When I left his place I was none too sober. Nothin' new there either. I hit a curb and had a flat tire out by the slaughterhouse. This cute young doctor...wait till you meet him...was getting off shift at Santa Paulina General and stopped to help me. I was so bedraggled. Honestly Joey, I looked like something the cat dragged in. He took me home for the night...or was it two. I've sort of lost count. Anyway, he patched me up. In all the excitement, he lost his cell phone, but that's the way it goes. Anyway, the good part is, we can't keep our hands to ourselves. He wants me to move in with him, so I've got to get going."

My anger had dissipated. Rory was Rory. What did I expect?

"Well, don't let him get away," I said. "We could use a doctor in the family."

"By the way, I'm sure you've heard the rumors. The good doc is going to take care of my problem. I can't have Colby Stafford screwing up my life for the next eighteen years."

"Don't tell me about it. I don't want to know."

"Up yours then," she said.

She grabbed her purse and was gone.

The moment the door slammed, I got a call from Chief Dunning down at The Precinct.

"I had the weirdest experience about an hour ago," he said. "Your sister's rich boyfriend paid us a visit with mud all over his nice cashmere overcoat. Says he was kidnapped by a gangster, a cop and a Catholic priest, who tried to murder him out by the old cannery."

"That's quite a story," I said.

"When that young blonde wouldn't back up his version of events, we laughed him out of the station house and sent her back to her parents in Spokane. Ever hear a more ridiculous accusation?"

My throat went dry. I swallowed hard.

"Never," I said. "He must have been delirious."

"By the way, Joey, how's Father Mick?"

"Fine."

"And your brother Pug, down at The Aces High?"

"Couldn't be better, Chief," I said, sweat popping out of my forehead.

"And yourself?"

"Still resting in bed like the doctor ordered."

"Well, me boyo, I suggest you stay there and give us all a rest."

TROUBLE IN GUNNAR

Mom was barely cold in her grave when Bell Jones began warming Dad's bed. Well, that's not entirely fair, being that Bell was no dummy and first made sure they tied the knot in front of Pastor Blevins, all legal-like.

I told Dad to get one of those prenuptial agreements like Tom Cruise and Donald Trump. After all, look what happened to Paul McCartney. Dad came into the marriage with a dairy farm and bank accounts and Bell came with a few faded dresses and a cardboard suitcase she kept under lock and key. He ignored my advice and told me I was far too cynical for a ten year old girl.

God knows where Bell came from and how she ended up attending our church. She certainly hadn't grown up in our small community of Gunnar. My big brother Robby and I tried to make the best of a bad situation, but, we were terribly lonesome for our real Mom.

The week Bell moved in Robby's dog Kelly was relegated to the barn. Allergies had never been mentioned during the brief courtship, but, my cat Sheba was the next family member to be evicted from the house. Mom's picture came down from over the fireplace and Bell's crabby ways drove away our friends.

We complained to Dad who said we had to make 'accommodations', that it was hard for someone new to step into a ready-made family. "It's none too easy for us either!" I said. He told me to watch the sass or he'd wash my mouth out with soap. I wanted to tell him that the soap thing went out with high button

shoes, but, I was already in enough trouble.

It wasn't long after Bell moved in that her brother Cal showed up on our doorstep. Whereas Bell was churchy and drab as an old dish rag, Cal was as hot as a pistol, tall and dark as a gypsy, with a casual manner and a deep farmer's tan. I decided to hate him from the get-go just because they were related. But, when Bell wouldn't give him the time of day and wanted him to hit the road, I decided he wasn't half bad. Before the first week was out I had a mad crush on him, even if he was twenty years older than me. What the heck, Grandpa was twenty years older than Grandma.

Cal had worked as a roustabout for Woodman's Traveling Circus until the operation went belly up. He was full of adventurous and hair-raising stories about life under the Big Top. Because he was a natural with machinery, including the milking machines, Dad let him bunk in the tack room.

One day when I was showing Cal which cows were easy and which ones were likely to kick his brains out, Bell flew into the barn and slapped me so hard in the face my ears rang.

"What the hell!" shouted Cal.

"Don't you dare interfere," said Bell, stabbing a finger so close to his face that he jumped backward and almost fell over a bale of hay.

Bell grabbed me by the hair and dragged me upstairs to my room. A 4-fingered welt spread like a red spider across my cheek. My knees were trembling and one of my teeth was loose.

"Stay the hell away from Cal," she said, her face so close to mine that my eyes wouldn't focus. "He's trouble."

"Mom never hit us," I cried. "I'm going to show Dad what you did to me," and I tried to push past her. She grabbed me by the arm and dug her nails in.

"You're not showing anybody anything. You're staying in your room for the rest of the day. You have a headache. Do you understand?"

"I DO NOT! Dad may think you're the cat's pajamas, but, I know better."

"Speaking of cats," she said, "can you imagine what a microwave could do to that little fleabag of yours?"

Robby crept up to my room after dark and I told him everything. "I don't know what I did that made her so mad."

"It's reverse magnetism," said Robby. "She hated you from day one. I'm going to take Kelly and Sheba over to the Hayden farm. Then we'll just have ourselves to worry about."

* * * * * * *

Dad was always with us in the evenings after the farm work was done. Bell was smart enough not to pick on me when he was around. We had no television, as Pastor Blevins believed it was a corrupting influence on society. I read aloud from Harry Potter, Dad recited Longfellow and Cal had us in stitches with his wild circus tales. But, Robby was the star of the show. At fourteen his voice had changed, and through his wooden dummy Jimbo, he could mimic the voice of a lumberjack, a two-year-old or an old lady. Bell proclaimed that ventriloquism was "of the devil", as it was never mentioned in the bible, and Harry Potter books were evil and promoted witchcraft.

A week later Jimbo disappeared and I found the ashes of poor Harry in the fireplace. There was a witch in the house, but, it wasn't Harry Potter.

In early June Dad became sick as a dog. He was plagued with stomach pain, fatigue, headaches and confusion. One day he called me Violet, but, Violet was his sister who drowned back in the 60's when they were kids. Soon he was bedridden. We all pitched in to pick up the slack. Cal tended the cows, Robby, always good at the forge, shod our draft horses, Bonnie and Clyde, and I made sure the shoats were fed.

Bell was always at Dad's side with her homemade lentil soup. In the Old Testament, Jacob cured his brother Esau with a 'pottage of lentils,' but, instead of improving, his symptoms got worse.

Bell prayed and placed her faith in the All Mighty, but, when

Pastor Blevins paid us a visit and saw how yellow Dad's skin was, he said that God in his grace gave us doctors and if Bell didn't take him to see one, he would.

Bell didn't like anyone telling her what to do, but, Pastor Blevins was a force to be reckoned with, and when he said 'jump' you jumped.

After Pastor Blevins was gone and Dad and Bell were on their way to town, Robby and I made a beeline for the attic. Jimbo had to be somewhere and we were sure as hell going to find him. We rummaged through the dust and cobwebs, sneezing as we went.

"Abby, look what I found!" I knew right away it was Bell's mysterious suitcase, the one we were forbidden to touch.

"Open it!" I squealed, plopping down in the dust beside him.

"Maybe it's full of money. I bet she's been holding out on us."

A hanger proved too awkward, but, Robby worked his magic with a bobby pin and the case popped open. He sat back on his heels with a groan. "Just some clothes," he said.

I pulled out a red satin dress, a pair of black lace stockings, a classy blonde wig and silver high-heeled sandals. "Look at this lingerie," I said. "She never wears anything like this for Dad."

I dug deeper and surfaced with a packet of documents. There was Bell's face on half a dozen driver's licenses under various aliases: Belinda Jenson, Bella Johnson, Becky Jackson.... "I don't think our new mother is who she pretends to be."

"Holy shit!" said Robby. "Look at this baby." He pulled a small, ivory-handled pistol from the bottom of the suitcase.

"It's too small to be real," I said.

"It's real all right and it'll shoot you just as dead as a big one. Look. It's loaded."

"Dad will kill us if he finds out we've been monkeying around with her stuff."

"He won't find out."

We heard the screen door slam downstairs.

"Cal!" we said, in concert, shoving everything back in the suitcase and slamming it shut.

We caught Cal raiding the fridge. Bell had very strict rules about the kitchen. The fridge and pantry were out of bounds to us peons.

"Busted!" laughed Robby.

"So put me on the Ten Most Wanted list," grinned Cal, a shock of black hair falling over one incredibly blue eye. "You two look like you've been rolling around in a dust bin."

"We were in the attic looking for Jimbo. We're not supposed to be up there," said Robby.

"Find anything interesting?"

"Just old junk," I said, quickly.

"Well, you don't tell on me, I won't tell on you." He stuffed half a pound of roast beef between two slices of rye. My stomach growled and Robby laughed.

"We're going to get in trouble," I said, raising an eyebrow.

Cal cut the sandwich four ways and gave Robby and me each a quarter. "If we're going to catch hell, we might as well be in for a dollar as a dime." He sat two big mugs of milk on the table and we all pulled up chairs. Cal pulled a beer out of his overalls pocket and popped it open with a hiss.

"Bell would kill you if she caught you bringing liquor into the house," said Robby.

"Can I have a sip?" I said. "Just to see what it tastes like."

"Come over here and sit on my lap," he said. I sat on his knee and he gave me a little sip out of the can. "Robby?" he said, lifting the can. Robby shook his head and gave me a warning look I chose to ignore. The beer didn't taste all *that* terrible and I loved being close to Cal, the sun-warmed feeling of his skin, his big protective arms.

"Just one more sip," I begged. He pressed the can to my lips and I drank far more than I'd planned to. I felt great, all relaxed and giggly.

"In only eight years I'll be eighteen" I said. "Grandma was only sixteen when she married Grandpa."

He gave me a gentle squeeze. "And when you're eighteen we'll run off to the circus together. I'll tame the lions and you

can walk the high wire."

"Promise?"

"On my honor," and he kissed me on top of the head.

I slid off of his lap and took a couple gulps of milk which didn't set all that well with the beer. I don't know how I could have been feeling so chipper one moment and....

Robby grabbed my hand and hurried me off to the bathroom. I gagged a couple times then collapsed over the toilet and upchucked.

"Whew, just in time," I said, giving him a goofy smile. The room began to spin and I sat down on the tile with a soft thud.

"I don't want you talking to Cal unless there's someone else around," said Robby. "It's not like we know anything about him."

"You're not my Dad. You can't tell me what to do." The green feeling swept over me again. I leaned over the toilet and threw up the rest of the beer.

* * * * * * *

We'd cleaned up all traces of our noontime bacchanal by the time Dad and Bell came back from Gunnar.

I threw my arms around Dad's waist. "Are you going to be okay? What did the doctor say?"

"He's working on it," said Dad, as Robby and I helped him to the bedroom. "It might be hepatitis or mono. They're running tests."

"You kids come and sit down at the table," called Bell. Cal sauntered in through the screen door and pulled up a chair. Bell opened the fridge. "Who's been into the roast beef? And the milk is almost gone!"

"It was me," I said, feeling mildly hung over and unusually fearless. I'm having a growth spurt."

"You must have a tapeworm!" she said.

I glanced at Cal who had a big grin on his face. I started to giggle and pretty soon Robby joined in. "I don't see what's so

funny," said Bell, which made us laugh all the harder.

During dinner I caught Bell staring at me with eyes as hard and cold as ice cubes. I'd upped the ante of hostility, but, my beer bravado was quickly turned to dread.

* * * * * * *

For the next couple of days I hung out by Dad's bedside or stayed close to Robby as he did his chores. One quiet afternoon when I thought Bell was in the henhouse she caught me foraging in the forbidden pantry. She grabbed me with her talons and began shaking me like a rag doll.

"I just want some lentil soup," I warbled, trying to keep my head from tumbling off my shoulders and rolling across the floor like a bowling ball.

"You know I make that soup for your father's recovery," she grated.

She was wearing another wilty cotton dress with a faded flour sack apron, her hair pulled back in an old maid's bun, a pair of shlumpy brogues on her feet. Mom had been so gay and colorful and fun and Bell seemed to bend over backwards to look like a frump.

"I don't know how Dad could have married such a dreary person. Mom was pretty and kind and you're as ugly as a warthog." Her fists started to fly but I'd already covered my head so my arms took the brunt of the blows. "You make me gag!" I shrieked.

"What's going on in there?" called Dad from the bedroom. Bell clamped a hand over my mouth.

"Abby saw a rat in the pantry, but, it's all taken care of."

"I hope so," said Dad.

"You make so much as a sounds and it's the last you'll ever make." said Bell, removing her hand from my mouth.

As I fled the pantry I tripped over a jug that stuck out from beneath the shelves, something that seemed strangely out of place.

Within minutes I heard Bell calling Sheba. "Here kitty, kitty, kitty!" I smiled as I walked out into the sunshine to lick my wounds.

* * * * * * *

Late that night Robby and I smuggled the jug of green stuff into the corn crib where we could examine the label by flashlight.

"Jesus, Abby, your arms are nothing but bruises."

"It's nothing," I said. "What does the label say?"

"Antifreeze."

My shoulders slumped. "Just that stuff that Dad puts in the truck."

"It has another name. Ethylene glycol. It's a deadly poison and I think Bell is putting it in Dad's soup. Do you ever remember him being sick before Bell came along?" I shook my head.

"What are we going to do?"

"I'm not sure yet. I need time to think."

We walked across the damp grass in our pajamas and slippers and hid the jug in the long-abandoned outhouse. "This should slow her down and give us time to come up with a plan."

* * * * * * *

The next morning Dad had a seizure at the breakfast table. I started to cry and Robby ran to the phone and called Dr. McBane who told us to meet him in the E.R.

Bell grabbed the phone and slammed it into the charger. "From now on stay off the telephone unless you have express permission to use it. I'm in charge here and I don't need the interference of children."

"I'll help you get Dad to the car," said Robby. "I want to have a word with Dr. McBane."

Bell put a hand on her hip. "Are you sick?"

"I didn't say I was sick. I simply...."

"You two stay here. You'll only get in the way. Make yourselves useful and help Cal stack the kindling."

Dad looked like he wanted to say something, but, no words came.

Hell with the kindling. As soon as the pickup was out of sight we thundered up the attic stairs. We needed those phony documents to make our case.

The suitcase was not where we'd left it. We scrambled around and pawed through the boxes in every corner.

"HEY, BABE, WHATCHA LOOKIN' FOR?" I nearly jumped out of my skin. It was Robby throwing his voice like he had before Jimbo vanished.

I punched him on the shoulder. "You scared me shitless!" I yelped.

"Pretty convincing, eh? I've been practicing at night in my room."

"Well, don't practice on me." I plopped into an old chair and a puff of dust exploded from the cushion. We spent another half hour searching the house and came up empty. "The suitcase is gone," I said. "That means she's on to us."

"Maybe so, but, we're on to her too. Let's call the E.R." I pressed my ear to the phone as Robby punched in a series of numbers.

"Emergency Room, Nurse Lindsay speaking. How may I help you?"

"I'd like to speak with Dr. McBane, please. This is Robby Granger and he's our family physician."

"One moment. The doctor is with Mr. Granger now, but, I could call Mrs. Granger to the phone."

"No, that's okay. I'll talk to her later." He quickly disconnected.

* * * * * * *

When Dad returned home with Bell that evening our hopes for his recovery dimmed.

"Why wasn't Dad admitted?" asked Robby. "He belongs in the hospital."

"What, you know more than the doctors now?" Bell shot back. "He's on antibiotics and he's been given fluids to balance his electrolytes." I had to admit he looked slightly better.

"What about the lab results?" I wanted to know.

"No Epstein-Barr, so mono is out. We're waiting for more results."

"What about a toxicology?" I pressed.

"My oh my, aren't we using big words. Maybe since you know so much you'd like to take over his treatment," scoffed Bell.

"Where in hell did you get those bruises?" said Dad.

"I'm going through an awkward stage, Daddy. Just ask Bell."

"Well, be more careful. You look like a washed-up boxer."

* * * * * * *

After I crawled in bed I heard Bell climb the stairs and open my door. I cringed as she sat on the edge of my bed.

"Have you been talking to Pastor Blevins about your Dad's illness?" she asked. "Or anyone else for that matter? Some things aren't to be discussed outside the family circle."

"No," I said. "What's to talk about?"

"Farms are dangerous places, Abby. Even for smart little girls who think they know it all. Kids get kicked by horses. They fall down wells. They lose their footing and tumble into empty silos. Sometimes, they simply disappear and no one finds their bones for 100 years. It would be a shame if something happened to a curious little girl like you."

That night I dreamed that Bell shot us all as we slept and took possession of everything Dad had worked for his whole life.

The next day we woke to thunderstorms and the power went out with a spray of sparks along the wires between the highway and the house. Dad seemed well enough to sit up in bed, so Robby and I decided to keep him company. I sat in a chair

beside his pillow while Robby went through his repertoire of voices. He did Auntie Pearl's dry cackle, Pastor Blevin's *basso profundo*, Cousin Ralphy's adenoidal wheeze and Cal's sexy baritone. By the time he took his final bow, the color had risen in Dad's cheeks and a bit of the old spark had returned to his eyes.

"That was amazing," he said. "I think Bell's already left to pick up my prescriptions, but, why don't you go get Cal? I'm sure he'd get a kick out of hearing your voices."

Robby headed for the door, but, I beat him to it, dashing out into the rain and splashing through the puddles.

I was dripping when I reached the barn. I wrung as much water out of my pigtails as I could and retied the bedraggled ribbons. The barn was shadowy and smelled of sweet alfalfa and fresh straw. Cal kept everything shipshape: cows milked, stalls cleaned, garden weeded. I don't see how we could have managed without him since Dad's illness.

It might have been a sound beneath the clatter of the rain on the metal roof or just a funny feeling that tickled along my spine, but, I stopped before I entered the tack room. Inside, Bell and Cal were speaking in whispers. My breath caught in my chest and I hid in an empty stall where I could see them, but, they couldn't see me. Mom had always told me that eavesdroppers deserved what they heard, but, my curiosity got the best of me.

As they talked, Cal ran his hand up Bell's thigh and kissed her neck. I expected her to slap his face, but, she seemed to like it.

"The old goat doesn't suspect a thing. Same with the hick doctor. It's the girl I worry about. That little brat could queer the whole deal."

A rumble of thunder exploded over the barn roof.

In one graceful movement Bell slipped out of her dress and let it flutter to the floor like a butterfly's wing. Her pale, naked body rippled with shadows. Those baggy dresses had concealed long, shapely legs, a slender waist and small firm breasts. Cal's

hands and mouth were all over her body. He kicked out of his jeans and stood there naked as a jaybird. His big hands cupped her buttocks and when he lifted her she wrapped her legs around his waist. She was like a feather in his strong arms as they began moaning and moving rhythmically, hypnotically, as if they'd entered a parallel universe. He pulled the pins out of her old-fashioned bun and a waterfall of cinnamon-colored hair fell in waves to her waist. Folding downward into the hay, the muscles of his back and shoulders flexed beneath a glistening patina of sweat. Bell writhed and laughed and purred like a kitten as her fingernails ran up and down his back.

This couldn't be the same joyless, mousy Bell who'd evicted me from the pantry. But it was. That drab exterior had been a brilliant, theatrical performance and we'd swallowed it hook, line and sinker. And Cal...this was the man who had held me on his lap and let me sip his beer and promised me...he'd promised me!

I flew into the house and ran past a startled Robby. I crawled into a corner of the attic and cried and cried. Robby came through the door and locked it behind him. I was heartbroken, shocked and confused. He sat down beside me and wiped my tears with his T-shirt.

"What the hell happened? Did Cal hurt you?"

"They were doing it," I sniffled.

"Who? What do you mean?"

"Bell and Cal. In the tack room. All naked. They were doing IT!"

"A brother and a sister? Are you sure?"

"Go look for yourself," I snapped miserably.

For a minute we sat together listening to the rain.

"What if they're not really brother and sister?" said Robby.

By the time we came down from the attic we'd formulated a plan.

The rain had stopped by dinnertime and the power had been restored. Bell warmed Dad's soup on the stove and poured it into a bowl.

"I think the soup should be tested," I blurted out. "It could be swimming with salmonella or botulism. Maybe Dad's allergic to lentils. Who knows?"

Suddenly, Bell stumbled and the soup went all over the kitchen floor.

"Now look what you've made me do!" she said. "And that was the last of it."

I gladly volunteered to clean up the mess.

I can't say it wasn't weird eating meatloaf and mashed potatoes like a Leave-It-To-Beaver family knowing what I'd witnessed that afternoon. Bell had slipped effortlessly back into her drab persona and Cal sat there like she didn't exist. Robby and I played it cool, but, the tack room antics had scrambled my ten- year-old brain. Later, I put Dad to bed with enough Benedryl in his hot chocolate to keep him under until the cock crowed.

At midnight Robby and I coasted the John Deere mower down the driveway to the highway, fired it up and drove the deserted mile to the Quick Stop. Once inside the phone booth, Robby dialed home and after a few rings Bell picked up.

"I gotta see you, baby. You were hot this afternoon," he said, in Cal's sexy rumble. The timber and resonance couldn't have been more convincing. "Slip away and meet me at Mike's Bar. And put on that red job. I'm tired of the weary, pioneer woman shit." Robby hung up before she could respond.

"What if she checks the tack room first?"

"Then we're screwed," Robby said.

When we got back the pickup was gone and Dad was still out like a light. I ran to the tack room and woke Cal. Despite everything I knew, he still made my heart flutter. But, my head was on straight. Well, almost straight.

I handed him the keys to Dad's old Ford. "Bell needs you to pick her up at Mike's Bar. The connection was bad, but, I think she's having trouble with the truck."

The moment he pulled onto the highway we called Pastor Blevins. Half way through our story he was out of bed and

dressed.

"I'm calling an ambulance for your Dad," he said. "In case Bell and Cal return, I want you kids with me."

* * * * * * *

Both of the vehicles were parked outside when the three of us entered the bar. It was a rowdy crowd and the baseball bat at Mike's elbow spoke volumes. Hank Williams warbled "Your Cheatin' Heart" from a bubbling jukebox, and everyone including Mike, ignored the NO SMOKING sign above the door.

"Stand by the jukebox and don't move," directed Pastor Blevins.

Cal sat at the bar looking like himself in his jeans and plaid shirt, but, if I hadn't seen the red dress and blonde wig in the attic, I wouldn't have been able to pick Bell out of a police lineup. Her eyes were made up Egyptian-style, her lips painted sports car red. No longer the faded hausfrau, she looked the part of a high class hooker.

"Bell Jones!" boomed Pastor Blevins' voice over the ambient roar. The room fell still as heads swiveled toward the action. Bell looked like she'd been zapped by a stun gun and Cal blanched to the pallor of chalk. Then, like a thief startled in a heist, she slid serpent-like from the stool and headed toward the door with Cal hot on her heels.

Suddenly, Bell spotted me hiding in the shadow of the jukebox and her mind snapped like a fresh carrot from Grandma's garden.

"YOU LITTLE BITCH!!!" she screeched. "YOU'VE RUINED EVERYTHING!!!" She reached beneath her satin skirt and pulled the tiny gun from a lacy garter, swinging it in my direction.

Cal shouted, "NO!!!" and landed a solid punch to her arm. Robby jumped in front of me as the bullet whizzed by my ear and shattered the window of the jukebox.

Enraged by the betrayal, Bell whirled around and plugged Cal point blank in the chest. There was a look of bewilderment on his face as he slumped to the floor.

A cowboy in a big hat spun around on his stool and casually cracked Bell on the wrist with his beer bottle as if he dealt with crazy women every day of his life. God knows there were enough of them around the watering holes of Gunnar.

The gun flew across the room, skidded through the cigarette butts and spilled drinks on the floor, and came to rest in the darkness beneath the pool table.

In my effort to become invisible I found myself wedged between the pinball machine and the wall. Bell spotted me and the rage that had simmered behind closed doors boiled over for all the world to see.

She pulled me from my hiding place by the ears and threw me to the floor, the stiletto heel of her silver shoe aimed at my heart. I rolled aside in time to see the heel crack away from the sole when it punched the concrete floor.

Out of the corner of my eye I could see Mike yelling into the phone. A frantic crowd had gathered around Cal and girls in tight jeans and cowboy boots were huddled together crying, screaming or looking on in stunned disbelief.

I dove under the pool table like an Olympic athlete. Bell grabbed my foot and my tenny came off in her hand. A trio of Jack Daniels bottles crashed to the floor when she sailed it over the bar.

Robby leaped on her back, a bronco buster on his first mustang. The blonde wig toppled off and I screamed. There was the old Bell, the cruel rictus of her mouth, the severe school-marmish bun. She bucked Robby into the wall and dragged me toward her by the cuff of my jeans. Hands around my throat, she hobbled upright on her uneven shoes, lifting me off the floor by my neck.

Pastor Blevins' bulk appeared like an avenging angel, Mike's bat gripped in his giant paws. He pulled back his swing, like The Babe before he lost himself in the booze. The bat pole-axed

Bell behind the knees. CRUNCH! Home run. She dropped like an empty sack and I tumbled half conscious to the floor. Bell lay in a whimpering bundle, lipstick smeared grotesquely across her face, black lace stockings in shreds.

I wobbled to my feet, clutching my tortured Adam's apple, watching the room come back into focus.

Cal!

"How long before that ambulance gets here?" yelled Pastor Blevins.

"It ain't comin'" called Mike. "They only got one and it's out to the Granger farm. They'll send over Sheriff Gunderson as soon as they figure out what strip club he's at."

I walked over and knelt beside Cal. Someone had unbuttoned his shirt.

"Hold on, Cal. It's only a little hole. Hardly any blood at all."

He reached over with great difficulty and took my hand. "There isn't any air in this room," he said.

"For God's sake, would somebody open the doors!" I cried.

"Your hand is so warm. Only eight more years," he whispered, with a wink. "Then we're going to...." The light faded from his blue eyes and there was no longer anyone home behind them.

I don't know why I still loved Cal, knowing he was in on the whole plot from the get-go. If he hadn't hooked up with the wrong woman things might have worked out for him. In the end he made the right decision. He chose me over Bell and it had cost him his life. I kissed him on the cheek and let go of his hand. There was one more thing I needed to do.

I knelt on the grimy floor where Bell lay crumpled like a broken doll. I wasn't good at hanging onto hate and I let it all go.

"Who are you?" I asked. "Where did you come from?"

She looked at me like a mental patient in fugue and struggled to get the words out.

"After all the aliases, and all the towns, and all the scams... how the hell should I know?"

Bell gave an ugly laugh

"You were my one mistake, Abby. I should have knocked you off first."

During the struggle she'd somehow managed to retrieve the gun. She clenched her jaw and pressed the barrel to my cheek.

"Robby!" I screamed.

Bell gave a derisive snort, jammed the gun into her mouth, and pulled the trigger.

CASH

Women! They were nothing but a game to Cash. Three months of pouring on the charm and Carly was in the bag. They'd done it all nice and legal and quiet; preacher, ring, cozy little out-of-the-way wedding chapel. He was looking forward to tomorrow, when everything she owned was going into both of their names; stocks, bonds, bank accounts. Carly was rich and beautiful. Too bad for her that she wasn't overly bright. If she was, she'd smell him out as the fleet-footed grifter he'd always been. By the time she was onto his game she'd be cleaned out, and he'd be a thousand miles away, licking his chops and counting his take.

He showered, shaved, and put on the open-necked blue shirt that showed a subtle shadowing of chest hair. A strand or two of bling around his neck, a splash of Ax, and he'd be ready to go to work on his next mark, the gorgeous Greta. But, he'd better be careful. Greta was sharper than Carly. He couldn't afford any missteps. Her ailing banker father was almost ready to kick the bucket. Then he'd be rolling in dough. Her dough, if he played his cards right.

A man could marry an endless succession of women, if he kept moving, used a phone book full of aliases, and never bothered with the inconvenience of divorce. As long as one wife never found out about the others (and that hadn't happened yet) he could run the same scam from here to kingdom come.

Cash smoothed back his head of black hair, allowing one renegade curl to fall casually over his forehead, like that cool actor

on the old *Hawaii Five-O*. 'You handsome dog' he thought, as he checked his image in the mirror, one last time. He smiled his crooked smile. He had a hard job, but, somebody had to do it.

He still had five thousand dollars in his wallet, money from the aging widow who was waiting for him in Tulsa. He snickered. It was going to be a long wait. He'd used what he'd had to bag Greta. He hoped it wouldn't take much more.

Carly was already in bed glued to American Idol. She looked up absently as he tried to slip unnoticed out of the door of their luxury condo. Yes, he could say 'ours', now that they tied the knot. He liked the way the word rolled around in his head like a billiard ball. 'Ours.'

"You're forgetting your wallet, darling," she cooed, from the acre of satin comforters. "I found it on the kitchen counter." He smacked his forehead with the palm of his hand. You get rushed, you start doing stupid things. As he reached for his wallet, that nasty little poodle of hers tried to bite his fingers off.

"Now, now Tiffany!" she scolded.

God, how he hated that pampered little rodent. He was already planning its mysterious disappearance.

He slipped the wallet into the same pocket with the red velvet ring box that held the big blue diamond that Carly had never seen. She pulled him down to the bed for a kiss. He had to admit she was a delicious babe. Golden hair. Skin like white chocolate. But, he wasn't in the game for love, or sex, or any of the usual clichés. He kept things simple. He was strictly a money man.

She planted a soft kiss on his lips. Gullible piece of fluff. Tiffany snapped and he jerked away.

"Sweetheart?"

Good lord, what now? He was never going to get out of here. His antiperspirant was already letting him down.

"Angel, I've got to meet a client. If I can close this deal, we can spend a whole month in Florida, soaking up the sun and living on nachos and Margaritas."

He could tell from the look on her face that she had something on her mind, if that was possible.

"Please, don't be mad," she pouted. "I went shopping this afternoon and the Porsche is out of gas. I pulled into the carport on fumes." He could swear the dog was gloating.

Cash felt like blowing his stack, shaking her by the hair, slapping her up. He'd certainly had enough practice. But, he wasn't going to blow his gig. Not tonight. He had to be patient, just a while longer, but all this patience was about to give him an aneurism.

Carly reached for her purse and dangled the keys to the station wagon. Next to the Porsche it was a junkyard on wheels. What did she think he was? A house husband with three kids and a cocker spaniel? This was the car she let the housekeeper drive when hers was broken down. Fine impression this was going to make on Greta.

"It's okay," she smiled sweetly. "I know you'll take good care of it."

Holding his temper was giving him acid stomach.

Cash glanced at his watch. He was running dangerously late for his dinner date. If he took the time to siphon gas out of the station wagon, Greta would be breathing fire by the time he picked her up and the whole scam would be ruined.

He jingled the Ford keys into his pocket and headed out the door. He'd tell Greta the Porsche was in for a tune-up and he had to borrow his cousin's wheels. He didn't actually have a cousin. In fact, he'd left everyone in his family down some long-forgotten road, so many years ago he could no longer remember exactly what they looked like. A dad with whiskey on his breath. A mother with a bad cigarette cough. They'd all be six feet under by now.

Greta took one look at the car, lifted her delicate eyebrows and said they'd take her Lincoln. She was as darkly exotic as Carly was golden, with shiny, long black hair and brown eyes deep enough to drown in. He left the Ford parked on the street outside her luxury high-rise. With any luck someone would steal it and save him further embarrassment.

It wasn't a very auspicious beginning for such an important

evening, but wait until she saw the ring. It was a rock the size of a watermelon and it was the real thing. Scored it from 'wife' number three. It had been on a dozen fingers in the last few years, but he'd always managed to get it back before he'd moved on.

He almost laughed out loud when Greta decided on the Fireside Lounge. He'd met both of them there on the same night, Carly during happy hour, Greta later in the evening after he'd dropped Carly back at her place. They ordered up a storm; shrimp cocktail, wilted spinach salad, rare prime rib, expensive French wine. Over Grande Marnier and cherries jubilee, he popped the question and she said, yes! yes! yes! and bubbled like a school girl.

The ring blazed like a small bonfire on her delicate finger. He leaned across the table, kissed her red lips, hugged her the best he could with the table between them. Her white diamond earring felt like an ice cube against his cheek and he could smell the hint of light lemony perfume on her graceful neck. April, she told him, would be the perfect time for a wedding. It was her favorite month and the lilacs would be in bloom. April. Only a few short months away. Victory! Greta was in the bag.

Just like when he was a kid, too much excitement and he had to take a piss. The check arrived, but he had to make an emergency pit stop, now! He left his credit card on the table so Greta could pay the check. Then she said they'd go back to her place and 'get naked.' Oh well, it was all in a day's work.

He didn't mind leaving the credit card. This way he didn't have to dip into the 'real' money. No one would ever make the connection between the fictitious name on the card and the real him, although there were times when he couldn't quite remember who the real him was.

He resisted the urge to strut and crow on his way to the head. He was consumed with fantasies of community property rights and joint bank accounts. Her daddy also had a yacht and a vacation home in the Bahamas. He could see himself kicked back in the shade of a veranda, sipping a mint julep. He decided right

then and there, his grifting days were over. Greta was a keeper. He was ready to settle down.

When he returned to the table, Greta had gone off to powder her nose, her black sequined purse snugged next to her wine goblet, right out in the open where any passing crook could make off with it. Twenty precious minutes passed before he discovered that the purse was full of Kleenex and the Lincoln was gone from the parking lot. His heart clenched violently in his chest. What the hell was going on here?

Dames were nuts! You never knew from one moment to the next what they were going to do. Her father. That had to be it. A medical emergency. The final one, if his luck held. Relax, Cash. It's all good.

Now the waiter was standing over him waving the check, tapping his foot. No, the lady had not paid. She'd run out of the establishment like her dress was on fire. He must be right then. A grave family crisis. Even so he'd feel a lot better if the diamond ring were in his pocket instead of on her finger.

The waiter cleared his throat. "Sir, the check."

Annoyed at having to dip into the 'real' money, Cash pulled out his wallet. Irritation in his every gesture, he flipped open the bill compartment. Empty! That was IMPOSSIBLE! The wallet hadn't left his pocket all evening.

The waiter snorted with disgust and went to get the manager.

Sweat prickled in Cash's armpits and ran down his ribs like spiders. Now, the manager was walking toward his table, looking none too friendly. Panic stricken, Cash bolted from the restaurant like a common criminal. Normally, he was smooth as silk, could talk himself out of these small fixes, but, with all the worry over Greta his mind simply vapor-locked.

Three blocks away he stopped running, his heart thundering in his chest. Shit! He was too old for this crap. Felt like he was going to have a heart attack. And just when everything was going so well.

Now what? He found a pay phone and fished for the last coin to his name. His phone rang and rang. Damn! Carly had turned

off the f-ing ringer again. Then he remembered that the Porsche was out of gas, so she couldn't have picked him up anyway. He hung up and the phone swallowed his last quarter. He beat the damn machine to death with the mouthpiece, only stopping after he crushed his thumb.

Desperate, he found himself pacing outside a liquor store. He hated this part of town. Reminded him of the kind of neighborhood he'd run away from as a scrawny, hungry kid. He was at his wit's end until he bumped into a good Samaritan named Blooper, who drank his beer out of a paper bag, and gave him a lift in an old, red pickup that smelled like marijuana and sweaty dogs.

When they pulled up to the high-rise, there was no sign of the Lincoln. He pushed Greta's buzzer a hundred times and got no response. In sheer desperation, he kicked the security door, until he snapped a toe. Back in the street, the Ford sat low to the ground on four slashed tires.

This kind of shit didn't happen on this side of town. This kind of shit didn't happen to him! The sick swirling in the pit of his stomach told him the engagement was off. It also told him his diamond ring was probably in another state by now, along with the exotic, erotic, black-haired Greta. He doubled over and threw up next to the Ford.

Blooper was leaning casually against his truck, rolling a doobie, spilling most of the bud onto the asphalt. He looked up with a shrug.

"Need a ride someplace else, bub?" he said.

It was pitch black with no moon on the rise. As lousy as he felt, it was a comfort to see the golden lamplight spilling from the condo window. It was nice to know that even if he didn't give a hill of beans about Carly, she'd greet him with open arms. He might even put up with that yapping rodent another day or two.

He slipped his key in the lock, wondering what cover story he'd concoct about the missing Ford. In a pinch he always came up with something. The condo was both quiet and empty. Carly

was nowhere to be seen. The satiny bed was made, but every last personal item had been removed from the rooms. The drawers, shelves, closets and medicine cabinet were empty and every surface was wiped clean. It was as if Carly had never set foot in the place. The only thing left behind was a vague scent of lemon in the air. Then he noticed the note pinned to the lampshade.

YOU CAN KEEP THE FORD.

Holy shit! The Porsche!

Cash ran down the stairs and limped toward the carport. The slot was empty. A small patch of transmission fluid shone wetly in the greenish glow from a street lamp.

When he roused the grumbling condo manager from his sleep, Cash's hair was a mess and he looked like a raving lunatic. There was no Carly Chase in his records and never had been. Condo 205 was owned by a couple who were vacationing in Europe for the last six month. Then the old goat accused him of being on drugs and went to call security.

Cash stood in the dark parking lot, immobilized by shock and disbelief. For the first time in his life he didn't know where to turn. Everything he'd worked so hard for was gone...the money...the diamond...the Porsche. How could this have possibly happened to him?

In a flash of indignation he had the fleeting impulse to call the cops; then again, he was embarrassed at having been taken. It would also have been a little complicated to explain. What if they asked him a lot of questions? What if they came up with his real name?

His best bet would be to make his way back to Tulsa. He turned his pockets inside out. He'd put through a call to the widow, but it would have to be collect.

AGAINST ALL ODDS

The first rumble of thunder rolled over Little Ireland as I blasted through the front door like the F.B.I. on a midnight bust. Mama jumped a foot off the couch, the extent of her day's exercise.

"Holy shit, Rosemary! I thought the Russians were coming." I tossed my books on a chair inside the door.

"Guess what? I'm the best speller in the Hoover class of '56. I get to compete in the countywide at Cooley next week. If I win, the cash award will cover my books at Community."

"With such big ideas you'll need all the help you can get. It's dark outside. Where the hell have you been?"

"In the library. I only have a few days to prepare. Alexa Micheluzzi almost beat me today. This is serious stuff, Mama."

"That rich girl from Country Club drive?"

"She's really very nice once you get to know her, but she doesn't need the money and I do."

"I'm surprised she didn't rig it."

"The spelling bee? How do you rig a spelling bee?"

"Rich people do whatever they want."

That's the way Mama was, always thinking someone was going to pull one over on her. The rich. The Jews. The teller at the bank. We lived in the shadow of the factories on Lower Division Street where Mama kept the windows closed against the smoke and the doors locked against the undefined adversary in her head. A few feet to the east and our house would be in the center of the railroad tracks. Across the street was the Rescue

Mission, the Thrift Store and the Tammany Hall Bar that used to belong to Old Da. We had money in those days, enough for center cuts and nice clothes.

Now we make due on Mama's disability checks.

"So, what was your winning word?"

I wanted so desperately to say verisimilitude, xylophone or mellifluous, words that sang with the color and music of language.

"Diarrhea," I said. "Miss Silverwein says it appears in almost every spelling bee." I worshipped Miss Silverwein with her soft wool suits, cultured demeanor and mist of Blue Waltz perfume. I wanted to be just like her, teach English when I got out of college and smell as sweet as a new doll fresh out of the box.

"Diarrhea," said Mama. "D-I-A-R-R-H-E-A. That's an easy one. It's right on the label of the Pepto bottle." Mama sometimes surprised me with all the things she knew. "I wouldn't broadcast it though. It's not a very ladylike word."

"At Countywide we have to come up with the spelling *and* the definition. It's much harder than what I'm used to."

"What if they give you fair? That could be county or bus."

"They won't. It wouldn't be fair. Get it?"

She'd lost interest in the subject and I found myself talking to the back of her head. She concentrated on her quiz show. The horizontal on the TV had been going crazy for two weeks and I was afraid she'd go blind if she didn't stop squinting at it. Time to break the bad news before I lost my nerve.

"Mama, I'll need a dress for the competition."

She stared straight ahead like she hadn't heard me. She'd been pinching pennies to fix the TV. She didn't want to hear about dresses. That was even worse than yearbooks and class rings, things I had yet to mention and probably never would.

"It's important, Mama. I'll be standing in front of the whole auditorium." "Phoenix," she said to the TV. "Capitol of Arizona." She rubbed her left foot. "My bunions are killing me. Wear the blue velvet Aunt Nora gave you for your birthday."

I was still talking to the back of her head. I stepped between

her and the t.v. so she'd have to look at me.

"That was three years ago! You passed it on to Cousin Virginia, don't you remember?"

Mama shifted her generous bulk and let go of her foot. The couch protested with a squeak of broken-down springs. She sighed heavily.

"Well, I guess we'll have to do something. Can't have you looking like the Shanty Irish now can we?" implying our roots were Lace Curtain, maybe Castle if we traced them back to Sligo.

When I looked at Mama, schlumping on the couch, stuck to the TV, adding another ten pounds every year like interest on a rich man's bank account, it's hard to believe she used to be called Irish Rose. Old Man Bulger's girl is a beauty. That Bulger girl is going places. Her eyes were a pale artificial-looking blue that amazed you at what nature could come up with and she still had shiny dark hair and perfect white skin, so I guess the stories are true.

Mama gave a deathbed sigh and I knew what was coming.

"I dreamed of becoming an airline hostess," she said, as rain began to rattle against the windowpane. There was no escaping the oft-repeated tale so I listened politely like it was the first time, no moaning, no rolling of the eyes.

"I know, Mama," I said.

"When I got pregnant in the eighth grade I told Old Da how Cousin Eddie had forced me. He made me swear on my rosary. Then he told me I had to put 'unknown' on the birth certificate where it says father's name. No need to shame the family. He'd handle it, he said. That Eddie Malone, he was a loose cannon but be was well-liked in the neighborhood. Slander his name said Old Da it could hurt business at The Tammany. Who gives a shit what a bunch of boozers think? Then Father Henry kicked me out of St. Bede's, and me on the honor roll, when everybody knew about him and Father Devlin. Hypocrites all of them. Never trust anyone in a position of authority. They're all corrupt."

I was supposed to say Whatever happened to Eddie? So I did.

"The next time I saw Eddie he had a broken nose, two black eyes and a missing tooth right up front. Looked like a pug gone down in the twelfth. That's the way the Irish took care of business back then. After that Eddie crossed the street whenever he saw me coming, like if he looked at my face he'd turn to stone, like I was the Medusa with a head full of snakes." She shook her head, her eyes softening, remembering. "Eddie looked just like a young James Cagney, all cocky and full of it. Funny thing is, with a little persuasion be could have had me the right way." Her blue eyes washed over me. "Dreams are a dangerous thing, Rosemary. Something always comcs up."

"You're scaring me Mama. Don't talk that way."

I stopped listening and ran through the study words in my head: sociolinguistic...metasomatism...nidifugous...phlogistic....

Pompous, pedantic words I'd probably never use. I simply wanted books for college so I could become an English teacher, wear nice clothes, go to the dentist if I had a toothache or to a Jerry Lee Lewis performance with enough money left over for a hamburger and a shake.

Rain clattered like gravel against the window. I walked across the tattered linoleum and looked into the gathering darkness. Mama was still talking, mostly to herself now.

"Someday I planned to change my name from Frances to Rosemary but there wasn't much point anymore so I gave the name to you. Then I sat on the couch, gave you your bottle and gained one hundred and fifty pounds," like giving me my baby bottle was what did it.

A flash of lightning x-rayed the bones of the cannery across the tracks. The TV crackled and went dark. "Now look what's happened?" said Mama. The rain fell steadily, silvering the rails in the light from the factories south of the crossing. She fiddled with the knobs on the front of the t.v. 'Son-of-a-bitch!'"

I couldn't help smiling. I shouldn't be hard on Mama. Between Eddie, Old Da and Father Henry what could you expect? At least she'd escaped the Irish disease when most of her family

had gone the way of the drink and the smokes, their livers pale and spongy, lungs plugged up like tenement plumbing. After the autopsy Dr. McBane said he could have tarred the interstate with the sludge in Old Da's lungs. Sometimes at night I sit by my bedroom window watching the green neon shamrock flicker in the window of The Tammany, expecting Old Da to push through the double doors, the cinder of his Lucky Strike burning like a red eye in the darkness, his pockets full of the night's receipts. He was always a happy man no matter what and when he died a light went out on Lower Division. The good times were done.

A freight rumbled through on the far side of our lot and the jelly jars rattled in the kitchen cupboard. Decades of vibrations had loosened the joists beneath my feet, a nail or two pushing through the linoleum to catch a toe. I watched the red lights of the caboose until the train rolled through the almond orchards on the outskirts of town and disappeared around a curve.

"I love the sound of that old train," said Mama. Yesterday she'd hated it, forever vacillating between praise and disdain at our location. "Reminds me we live on the right side of the tracks. Yes Ma'am, the last house on the right side of the tracks," like our house with its chipped paint and sagging porch was a notch above the other rotting structures on Lower Division. "These buildings are all historical. Pretty soon they'll be on the National Register."

Sally's mom hadn't seen it that way. Sally who said she'd be my best friend forever and ever. The last time she came to my house her mom had a cat fit.

"I don't want you hanging around that Bulger girl. That neighborhood has gone to the dogs. Have you seen what's become of Frances?" THAT GIRL! THAT NEIGHBORHOOD! FAT PIG! TUB OF LARD!

Sally pretends she doesn't know me. If I sit at the same table in the cafeteria she leaves. She thinks she's better than me even though I'm smarter and get better grades. I could knock her down a peg or two if I thought it was all her fault, tell her that

her mom is in bed with Jimmy O'Toole on the nights she's supposed to play Bingo at the church. But then I'd make trouble for Jimmy whose wife already causes him enough grief.

Because of Sally's mom I don't let people come here anymore. No sleep-overs, no birthday parties, no studying with friends. It's the Rosemary at school I want people to know. The smart girl. The best speller in the class of '56.

Another clap of thunder and the lights go the way of the TV. "Why does this always happen to us?" says Mama.

Of course the lights are out in the whole neighborhood, even at the cannery until the generators kick in. Mama hoists herself off the couch and goes to her room. I light a candle and study my words late into the night...consanguinity...tourniquet... circumjacent....

On Saturday morning Mama robbed the cookie jar and we took the cross-town to Robert Hall's in the new strip mall. I held several dresses up to the mirror. When I saw the ruby red dress with the full skirt and puff sleeves next to my dark hair I knew it was the one. At twelve dollars and fifty cents plus tax it was more expensive than the others but Mama said I could have it provided I also wore it to the prom without complaint. She couldn't put herself through this shopping business twice in one year.

Forbidden Planet was playing at the Bijou but the Paradise was closer and Mama's feet were giving out. We saw *The Man Who Knew Too Much*. Doris Day was a singer who married James Stewart, a doctor. If I became a teacher I figured my chances of marrying a doctor were as good as hers. He could fix Mama's bunions and we could move to the other side of town, kill two birds with one stone.

After we shared a medium popcorn and a small Coke there was just enough money to catch the bus back home. I felt happy about the dress but sad for Mama. She'd have to start saving all over again to fix the TV. We were in for a long stretch of macaroni and cheese dinners.

At night I dropped into bed whispering my mantras. They'd

bring me more luck than my bedtime prayers ever did.... Dear God, make Mama happy...help her lose those extra pounds... make the roof stop leaking...make us rich...bring Old Da back... cypsela...perborate...surveillance....

"You're doing well," said Miss Silverwein. "Keep studying. Take another look at hemorrhoid and macedoine." A cloud of Blue Waltz perfumed the air, her fingernails clean and polished as she turned the pages of the study list.

"Normotensive. Thromboplastin. Zabaglione. Nobody's ever heard these words, let alone know what they mean. Are you sure the bee is going to be this hard?"

"We'll know soon enough. That's enough for today. Be sure you have appropriate attire for the competition."

I described the red dress.

"As long as it's not too fancy. This is a spelling bee not a beauty contest." She glanced at my shabby saddle shoes. "Look at those tiny feet. They can't be more than a six."

"Five and a half."

"Be sure to tell your mother that you need decent shoes to go with the dress."

I take my shoes off and carry them when it rains so the stitching won't go bad but I'd been wearing them the whole school year and they looked like The Wreck of The Hesperus. Besides, saddle shoes don't go with a party dress and my good Sunday shoes had gone the way of the blue velvet. Even without the movie there'd have been no money for shoes. The competition was about the words not my shoes. I'd make do.

After school Tommy Nolan helped me run through my words in the quad. The day I won the senior bee his finger-whistle left my ears ringing.

"I don't want to see you talking to that Nolan boy," Mama would say. "He lives on that unpaved road by the packing house. Stay on your own side of the tracks."

I ignored her and continued to see Tommy right out in the open. She sounded just like Sally's mom. I knew what she was thinking, but Tommy was no Eddie Malone.

It was dark and raining again when Tommy left me in front of my house and disappeared over the railroad tracks. Uncle Pete's patrol car was parked in front of The Tammany so I walked across the street and pushed through the double doors. Cooney looked up from behind the bar.

"Well, if it isn't the spelling bee queen. You made the morning paper, you and the five from the other high schools."

"How you doing Cooney?"

"Same-o, same-o."

"Hi baby," said Uncle Pete, turning toward me on his bar stool. "Come sit," and he patted the stool next to his. I slid in beside him. I felt more comfortable in the smoky dark interior than I did at home. A couple guys from the packing house were playing pool beneath a green-shaded ceiling fixture, the juke box at the back of the room bubbling red and blue, Green Door playing softly in the background. When I was little Old Da let me play the pinball machine and sleep in the back room until he locked up for the night.

"That kid's a minor," said a butinski at the other end of the bar.

Uncle Pete spun around, his badge glinting on the front of his blues.

"Shut your fuckin' gob or I'll shut it for you," he said. "She's family." The man went silent, dropped his shot glass into his mug of beer and watched the dark whiskey web through the golden bubbles.

"Boiler maker?" asked Uncle Pete. I laughed and shook my head. "Well then, finish off my beer. Not enough there to fill a thimble. Cooney, another cold one."

I sipped the beer. Before I knew it I'd downed two tall ones.

"Frances got you tied in knots?"

I nodded.

"She's a wet blanket. Don't let her get to you. Any time you want to move in with me and Rose, you're welcome."

"Thanks Uncle Pete. I'll be okay. The walls were beginning to close in, that's all."

An hour later he helped me across the street. I flopped on top of my bed and went down for the count...no dreams...no prayers...no words....

On the evening of the countywide I came down with the flu. One moment I was burning up. The next I was shivering with chills. Mama took my temperature. Normal. I had a debilitating case of nerves. I washed down two aspirin just in case.

To make things worse I was obsessing about shoes again. I took thick polish to the black saddle part and made a terrible mess of it. The whiter I made the shoes the dirtier the laces looked, one with a double knot where it had broken. I considered polishing the laces. I had lost my mind. No matter what I did I couldn't make saddle shoes go with a party dress. And all this time trying to keep the words in my head...ayahuasca... hyaluronidase...reconnaissance....

No question that the ruby red dress was stunning, the perfect color, the perfect fit. I stood in front of the mirror, refusing to look at my feet. I judged myself 99% okay.

Mama gave me change for the bus. She had a car and a license but could no longer fit behind the steering wheel. She wasn't coming with me. Her feet were acting up. More likely she didn't want to be seen in her slippers and faded muumuu the size of a circus tent. When you're fat or wear bad clothes people never look deeper to find out who you really are. I was sick with disappointment and giddy with relief. It was one less thing to think about. My head was crowded. I had trouble keeping the words inside...provocateur...conflagration...insouciance....

I slipped the change in the pocket of my tweed coat. It didn't go with the party dress but I'd ditch it as soon as I got to Cooley. Mama smiled and looked me up and down, trying hard not to look at my shoes. She hugged me. Her cheek was wet with nervous perspiration, rehearsing what she'd say when I failed. The flu was on me again. A deadly strain.

I opened the door and froze.

There stood Miss Silverwein in a gray silk suit and gold earrings, her hand raised to knock, a shoe box under her arm.

My legs began to collapse beneath me. I blanched.

"What are you doing here?" It was an accusation.

She looked surprised. Gave me a questioning look.

"Who is it, dear?" called Mama.

All the big words tumbled out of my head, tangling in the dirty, knotted laces of my shoes.

THAT GIRL! THAT NEIGHBORHOOD! FAT PIG! TUB OF LARD! Those were *my* words. Those were the ones that stuck. I stood there paralyzed.

"It's Rachel Silverwein, Mrs. Bulger, Rosemary's teacher."

She looked past me into the living room with its hopeless linoleum and tattered window shades, the living room where Mama's fat overflowed the couch cushions like bread dough rising in the oven—sweaty, fat bread dough, and the bunions on her feet as big as walnuts.

"Well, come on in."

Miss Silverwein's eyes flicked to my face. Catatonic. C-A-T-A-T

"I wish I could Mrs. Bulger but we'll be late. Maybe another time."

Her arm was firm around my shoulders as she rushed me down the stairs to the car. She opened the passenger door and put the shoe box on my lap when I sat down. She walked briskly around the hood, got in the driver's seat and felt my forehead.

"You're awfully warm, Rosemary."

"I'm sick. I'm going to throw up." I began to cry noiselessly, tears running down my cheeks, no sound except my uneven breathing.

An ice age passed.

"What I've heard is true then," said Miss Silverwein, giving me her full attention.

"What do you mean?" I licked a tear from the corner of my mouth.

She extended her hands, palms up. "The Irish don't know how to have a proper cry. Take the Italians or the Jews. They know how to bawl, how to wail, how to really let her rip. You

should have heard my mother when she dropped the Passover kugel on the kitchen floor. You'd have thought someone shot her cat."

I sputtered a laugh.

"That's better. It's clear I've been pushing you too hard. Everyone falls apart before a big competition, releases some of the stress. Really, it's not such a bad thing." She handed me her hanky all lacy and sweet with Blue Waltz perfume. I wiped my eyes and took a couple ragged breaths. "You can hang on to it," she said. "Go head, try on the shoes."

Inside the box was a beautiful pair of black leather flats like something Audrey Hepburn would wear. They smelled like the leather seats in Miss Silverwein's new Pontiac Strato-Streak. I took off my saddle shoes, pushed them underneath the seat and put on the new ones. They fit like soft kid gloves.

"Thank you. I love them. I'll pay you back. I promise. But, I'm sick. I really can't do this."

"Let's just drive a little then. I'll take you home anytime you want. Just say the word." She pulled a u-ey and driving slowly headed in the general direction of Cooley High. She turned her head to the left, her eyes running down the 700 block of Lower Division Street all wet and dreary, a few bums huddled against the side wall of the Stag Hotel For Men. "See that building with the blue and orange awning?"

"You mean Polly Prim Bakery?"

"I was raised in the apartment above the store. I played hopscotch on that very sidewalk."

"No kidding?" I was stunned. Lower Division? And yet she'd somehow gone from there to here.

"Sometimes I miss the old neighborhood but time marches on. First you live the life people make for you. Then you move forward and live the life you make for yourself." She placed her hand on my forehead. "Are you feeling any better?" I nodded. "You'll be fine, Rosemary. Tonight is a challenge but it's supposed to be fun. Make the most of it."

In the packed auditorium I saw Tommy, Uncle Pete and

Aunt Rose, at least a dozen cousins and teachers from all five competing schools. Once I nailed the first word...discompose... the flu had run its course.

After an hour and a half only two of us were left standing. My final adversary was Wang Lu from Chinatown, the one contestant everyone said could never win. He was a goofy kid, a head shorter than I. He wore sad black pajamas that were worn in the knees, cloth shoes and a bowler hat too big for his head. On our way into the auditorium a bully from Hoover, whom we all hated, gave his pigtail a vicious tug. His broken English was almost indistinguishable from Chinese.

Most of the words were easier than the ones I'd studied: misjoinder...raconteur...substratum...misspell...erudite...and the dreaded diarrhea. The definitions came easily. But, like Mama said, something always comes up, and this time it was the word uxoricide. Never heard it. Thought I could spell it. Had no idea what it meant.

"Uxoricide," I said. "U-X-O-R-I-C-I-D-E." So far so good. Icide. Icide. Icide. My head spun. Pesticide. Homicide. Matricide. Had something to do with murder. But, what the heck was an ux? Time was running out. Latin. Think Latin. It wasn't until I decided to give up that Et Ux leapt across a synapse in a remote fissure of brain. It rose like a bubble from the depths and broke the surface with a pop. Et Ux. I'd seen that somewhere. Old Da's deed to the house. The property belonged to Patrick Edwin Bulger, Et Ux. Et Ux had to be Grandma. Three seconds to go.

"The act of murdering a spouse," I said, just under the buzzer.

There were gasps from the few people in the audience who were familiar with the word. The English teacher from Cooley held up a hand for silence.

"I'm sorry, Miss Bulger. That is incorrect. Mr. Lu. Uxoricide."

I held my breath. If Wang Lu missed the word we'd go on to the next word and I'd still be in the game.

Wang Lu's father leaned forward in his front row seat looking anxious and hopeful. I looked at Miss Silverwein, who smiled and gave me a wink. Lu was trembling. "Uxoricide. U-X-O-R-

I-C-I-D-E. The act of murdering a...a...wife," he said. A moment of utter silence followed.

"That is correct young man. Congratulations, Mr. Lu." I thought he would faint. I congratulated him and shook his small cold hand. His father had tears in his eyes.

"You provided him with most of the answer," said Miss Silverwein on our ride home. "I suppose you're aware of that." It was still raining and the click of the windshield wipers made it hard not to fall asleep. During the competition I'd forgotten about the dress, the shoes....everything but the words.

"He won fair and square," I said. "I can work this summer to cover my first year at Community. It'll get me out of the house."

"How do you feel? You did great you know."

"I sweated in my new dress. I hope it's still okay for the prom."

"What word did you stumble on?" asked Mama, as I hung my new dress in the closet and slipped into my jeans.

"Uxoricide. I spelled it but didn't know the definition."

"That's an easy one, Rosemary, like when Cousin Eddie shot Nonnie and did seven to ten in the State Pen."

"My memory doesn't go back that far, thank God."

"Old Da told him before he married that girl that she'd slept with every shanty Irishman this side of Shannon Street. You couldn't tell Eddie nothing. Not a damn thing."

I laughed out loud and hugged her.

"So, who beat you, that Jew boy they call Little Einstein?" I put my new shoes on the closet shelf so they'd be nice for the prom and stepped into a pair of worn tennies.

"No Mama, it was Wang Lu from Chinatown."

"Chinatown? You mean you couldn't beat out a foreigner? They smoke opium, eat their cats."

SMOKE OPIUM! EAT THEIR CATS!

"Oh, Mama."

I put on my rain jacket and ran a brush through my hair.

"Get your coat. We're meeting Uncle Pete and Aunt Rose across the street. Cooney ordered a cake to celebrate my big

day."

"Pete, Rose, and all those Shanty Irish brats of theirs. I'm just not up to it."

"Here's your coat. Put it on."

"Rosemary, my bunions are killing me."

"You're coming if I have to carry you."

I worked at the shoe store in the strip mall that summer. I read *Peyton Place* by Grace Metalious, *The Color Curtain* by Richard Wright, and every book the Catholic Church told me to stay away from. I paid my own way to Community College and finished my degree on a scholarship to State.

The next time I saw Miss Silverwein she was Mrs. Adler and I was Mrs. Nolan. She sat at a table in Stenglers drinking a latte and reading a book with the morning sunlight on her salt and pepper hair. She wore a new perfume, something spicy and expensive.

"Miss Silverwein?"

She looked at me over her glasses. There was no sign of recognition in her expression.

"I'm sorry," I said. "It's been awhile. I'm Rosemary Bulger. The spelling bee? The new shoes? Uxoricide?"

The light went on in her eyes.

"Oh my God, Rosemary! How are you. You look wonderful. I imagine you're teaching these days."

"I changed my major. I'm a social worker. My husband Tommy is a civil rights lawyer. We're getting ready to leave for Mississippi to help with the voter registration drive."

"You're sure you want to stir up that hornet's nest? Do be careful."

"We will!' I laughed. "What are they going to do, shoot us?"

"Last I heard your mother wasn't doing well."

"I lost her a year ago. It was her heart," and Eddie Malone and the 'unknown.'

"I'm sorry, dear. Why don't you sit?"

I took the chair across the table from her.

"May I ask you a question?" I said. "You told me something

on the evening of the countywide. It helped me get through the competition" and more, much more.

"Shoot."

"Did you really grow up above the bakery on Lower Division?"

"Did I say that? I spent my entire childhood on Lighthouse Hill."

"You LIED to me!"

Her eyes danced.

"It was true as long as it needed to be. Aren't I terrible?" she said, and laughed and laughed.

LAST CHANCE IN GUNNAR

My eleven-year-old brother Duke Wayne and I lit out of the trailer as soon as the ashtrays started flying. We hid in the pickup in the carport as neighbors gathered at the curb in gossipy knots. It's hard when you're a kid and people think you'll never amount to a hill of beans. It's not like we picked Heidi and Gaylord out of the social register. We got stuck with our parents just like they got stuck with us. Deputy Wittler pulled up in his patrol car, the light bar flickering red and blue on the pocked metal skin of the trailer. He'd been here so many times that we called him Jason like he was a member of the family. He ignored the sounds of fighting and breaking glass and walked straight over to where we were hunkered down on the bench seat.

"What got 'em going this time, Bossy?"

Bossy, that's what they call me because Evangeline sounds like an old granny in her rocking chair. For now I'm stuck with it, but someday I'll change it to something fancy like Cheyenne or Turquoise.

"Gaylord gave her money for groceries and she bought a bottle of gin and a blonde wig. We have half a box of Lucky Charms and a pint of sour milk." Jason exhaled noisily and shook his head. Duke Wayne sat bottled up with his arms crossed over his chest, muscles knotting in his jaw. He wasn't much for letting off steam but I think things bothered him real deep.

Heidi was my worst nightmare but Gaylord was no prize either. At least he never whooped me with the buckle end of the

belt like Heidi does. When she isn't mad at us kids she's ragging on Gaylord for having the seven-year itch for all twelve years of their marriage. He says it's beyond his control, that when he steps into his cowboy boots and button-fly jeans and rolls that pack of Camels in the sleeve of his Budweiser t-shirt the ladies around the watering holes of Gunnar just can't keep their hands to themselves.

"Let me see your back, Bossy," said Jason.

"Not again," I moaned.

"It's either me or that old bat from CPS."

I dutifully pulled up the back of my shirt so he could have a look at the latest pattern of bruises.

"Those cigarette burns are from before," I reminded him. "Heidi told the social worker it wouldn't happen again."

"So she threw you back in the ring for one more round."

The trailer door burst open and Gaylord shot onto the dirt patch out front. He was bleeding from a cut on his forehead. Heidi stood in the doorway, a cigarette dangling from her lips. She wore silver spike heels with a tattered bathrobe and the chain of a silver fish scale purse looped around her wrist. When I saw her like this, with her hair all tangled and mascara smeared beneath her eyes, it was easy to forget how beautiful she was when she was all dolled up and sober. She swung a gin bottle and let it fly, but instead of hitting Gaylord it exploded against the door of the patrol car. Jason stiffened but kept his cool.

"Well, that's one she won't be drinking," said Gaylord, sauntering over.

Heidi lost her footing and ended up in a heap below the stoop. She looked toward the truck with eyes that refused to focus.

"You kids get in there and clean up that mess."

"You stay right where you are," said Jason. He walked over and slapped the cuffs on her small wrists as a second patrol car pulled up and Deputy Barnswallow got out.

"Take Mrs. Draper in and let her sleep it off," said Jason.

"How about him?" said Barnswallow, nodding toward

Gaylord.

"He's sober enough, I guess. Get something out of the trailer that she can be released in. Can't have her walking through town in her nightgown."

The neighbors clapped and whistled when Barnswallow pulled away from the curb with Heidi banging her head against the side window like a crazy woman. Her eyes were glassy and a cut opened above one eye.

Jason turned to Gaylord. "So, what's your plan for these young'uns?"

"Well, we're not going back in there," he laughed. Big joke.

"You're not driving anywhere either."

"I'll walk over to the Stardust for the night."

"What about the kids?' I won't have 'em sleeping in the back of the truck."

"They'll work something out with one of the neighbors. They always do."

Gaylord leaned into the truck window. He ruffled my hair and gave Duke a playful punch on the shoulder. "I'm not fit company right now," he said, with a lopsided smile. "I'll hook up with you and your mom tomorrow."

I watched him walk into the October night toward the lights of Centennial Blvd, the dead leaves swirling around his ankles until the shadows swallowed him up.

"We have school in the morning," I said. "My homework's in there."

"I'll go get your stuff," said Jason. "You kids got two choices. Either I release you to a responsible adult or it's CPS again."

Duke looked up. There was a spark of determination in his dark brown eyes. "I want to go to Uncle Dan's," he said.

* * * * * * *

Dan was standing beneath the porch light when we pulled up in front of the ranch house. Duke walked into the house with his baseball glove and bat, me tagging along with our school books.

Jason sat our box of clothes inside the door.

"How long this time?" asked Dan.

"She'll be out mid-morning." said Jason.

"Fair enough."

Dan Wellstone was a respected figure around Gunnar. He took pride in raising tough-as-nails cattle on the piss-poor homestead that had been passed down through his family. Heidi said he was a handsome sort if you liked the noble over-the-hill type.

Dan had light green eyes and an old-fashioned handlebar mustache that he kept neatly trimmed and waxed. I'd never seen him in anything but work clothes and a big cowboy hat but he kept a suit in the closet for funerals and jury duty. When Heidi and Gaylord went on a toot, he'd take us out to the ranch until things settled down.

That night the wind blew hard and cold off the reservation that backed onto the ranch. Sand and tumbleweeds piled up against the back of the house. He fed us stew and biscuits from an iron pot on the wood stove and settled us in blankets by the fireplace like pick-of-the-litter pups.

The next day Duke and I got off the school bus in front of the trailer park. The pickup was gone from the carport and Mrs. Raley, the park manager, was sweeping broken glass out of the coach door into the dirt. Liquor fumes drifted out to the sidewalk.

"What's going on Mrs. Raley?" I asked.

"What does it look like?" A metal curler popped out from beneath her flowered scarf.

"Where's our parents?"

"I have no idea," she said, with angry tears in her eyes. "You people are out of here. You can tell that dad of yours that I'll see him in court. This coach is ruined."

"We can help you clean it up," said Duke.

She shook the broom at us and we backed away. "It's people like you that give trailer trash a bad name."

"I'm a straight-A student, Mrs: Raley. I'm not trash," I said.

"Just wait a couple years," she said.

"Come on," said Duke, "before the old witch climbs on her broom."

We ran until we came to the truck stop in front of the Silver Spur Cafe. After asking around a bit we hitched a ride with a trucker who was pulling a load of hogs to New Mexico. He showed us tattoos he'd got in seven states and said he was shooting for all the lower forty eight. He pumped his brakes and let us out in front of the mailbox.

When we came to the top of the driveway, Dan was knocking dirt off a shovel against a fence post. He wiped the sweat off his forehead with a blue bandanna.

"Don't go behind the barn," he said. "I killed me a mean old rattler and where there's one there's bound to be more."

"We been kicked out of the trailer," said Duke. "The truck's gone and nobody's there."

"It's three o'clock," I said. "Has Heidi come by?"

"Not yet. Why don't we call the jail? Maybe they're going to hold her one more day."

We walked up the path toward the house.

"One more thing," said Dan. "I don't want you kids hitching anymore. Even after your parents pick you up, you need a ride, you call me."

Dan put in a call to the jail but they said Heidi had been released about eleven that morning.

"If the truck is gone I Imagine she hooked up with Gaylord," said Duke.

"Even if they pick us up we can't go back to the trailer," I said.

"I think we better make up the beds in the extra bedroom," said Dan, "Just in case. Now, who wants to help me put the new water pump in the truck?" Dukes eyes lit up. Mine did not.

"I'll make up the beds," I said.

That night at dinner I ate so much chili and cornbread it was downright painful to breathe. It was dark by the time I finished drying the dishes and Heidi and Gaylord still hadn't come. I felt an unsettling mixture of concern and relief. Uncle Dan didn't

have a TV or video games but I could sleep through the night without Heidi dragging me out of bed by my hair to clean up the trailer or see Duke Wayne get a whipping just because she was in a bad mood. Dr. Moss said that Duke was the youngest ulcer patient she'd ever seen.

"Get your jackets," said Dan, reaching for his hat. "We'll drive into town, see if that new water pump does the trick."

The manager at The Stardust Motel said Gaylord checked out early and headed in the direction of the trailer park, so we decided to check out the bars along Centennial Blvd...the Do Drop Inn...The Cave...The Dead Man's Hand. We were standing outside the Leprechaun Lounge, plum out of ideas.

Uncle Dan looked up and down the strip and gave his mustache a thoughtful twist. "I don't think we'll find them until they want to be found."

Duke became quiet. He looked at me, then at Dan, then at me again.

"You two have the very same shade of green eyes," he said.

"I think you're right," I said. "Same color as Mrs. Raley's cat."

"Don't that beat all," said Uncle Dan. "Bossy takes after her Mom's side of the family, just like you take after Gaylord's." We walked back and got in the truck. "How about a nice big piece of pie at The Silver Spur?"

* * * * * * *

A month later an envelope came from Gaylord. It had arrived at the trailer park before it was forwarded to the ranch. He said he'd been working at The Lucky Friday Mine in Idaho's Silver Valley. A one hundred dollar bill was enclosed.

"That's weird," said Duke. "Heidi can't be with him if he thinks we're still at the trailer park."

Dan made an effort to track him down, but when he reached the office at the mine, he was told Gaylord had headed up to Post Falls with a Shoshone woman.

Dan smoothed out the one hundred dollar bill on the kitchen table.

"Well," he said, "it won't put you kids through college but we could splurge at that big bookstore in Phoenix."

The bookstore was bigger than some of the dusty little towns I'd been in. I got a book on raising rabbits and Duke got one on repairing farm equipment. We had dinner at Denny's before heading back to the ranch.

A week after our trip to Phoenix, Deputy Wittler pulled up in his patrol car, sending a big dust cloud over the corrals. Duke was fiddling with the engine of an old tractor and Dan and I were throwing down some flakes of hay for the horses.

"Any word on Heidi?" asked Dan.

"That's what I was going to ask you," said Jason.

"Not word one on Heidi but Gaylord is up Idaho way."

"We gotta do something permanent about them kids. Can't have CPS crawling down my neck, Mr. Wellstone."

"Seems to me they're doing right fine where they are. I feed 'em right and their grades are up."

"You seem to be the only relation they got."

"Seems so."

"Their uncle, right?"

"That's a fact."

"And which side of the family would that be on, sir?"

The men stood in silence for a moment, their eyes locked and unwavering. The way they looked at each other made me a bit edgy.

Finally Uncle Dan said, "I'm closest to the mother."

Jason looked at the toe of his boot and kicked up a puff of dust.

"That's good enough for me, Mr. Wellstone. Have you considered filing a missing person's report on Heidi?"

"Couldn't hurt."

"Let's give it another week or so. I'd hate to do all that paperwork and find out she was just shacked up somewhere."

That Christmas Duke got a fully loaded tool box and I got

a breeding pair of Australian rabbits. We got new coats and gloves and riding boots. We saddled up and rode out to Blue Canyon and ate canned chili around a campfire. It was the best Christmas we ever had.

The winter months passed slowly like winter always does. One morning Duke and I rode the horses through a light snowfall to the mailbox at the end of the driveway.

"If they come back, I'm not going," said Duke. I knew what he meant.

"Me neither," I said. "I never want to leave the ranch."

He looked toward the horizon. "I want to see the world."

Dan took us to see Dr. Moss when my burn scars started acting up. They got worse in cold weather and before it rained, just like old people's creaky joints.

Duke's ulcer was healed, but he often cried out in his sleep and woke in a cold sweat. Dr. Moss prescribed ointment for my back and told us kids to go to the waiting room while she had a word with our uncle. I listened on the other side of the door.

"God knows what psychological damage those miscreants have inflicted on those children," she said. "If they return I'll have them incarcerated."

When they neared the door, I jumped into an orange plastic chair and snatched up a magazine.

"*Mechanics Illustrated*?" said Dan, when he saw me.

"It's more interesting than you might think," I said.

"Especially when read upside down."

Duke laughed so hard he almost fell off his chair.

It was a relief to have Heidi out of our lives, but given that Gaylord was more shiftless than down right mean, I missed his bad jokes and the way he used to ruffle our hair. Then, as the years passed, all I could recall was a man disappearing into a wind-swept night and a wild-haired woman thrashing her head against a patrol car window.

It was the summer between eleventh and twelfth grade when I drove the pickup into the yard and saw a woman with long black hair drinking from the hose in the garden. There was a

bedroll and backpack at her feet. She paid me no mind. I figured her for an illegal seeking shade and made no acknowledgment as I walked past her into the house.

A man sat at the table with Dan. Something about him looked vaguely familiar.

"Say hello to your dad," said Dan. I was caught off guard and couldn't think of anything intelligent to say. He looked half the size and twice the age of the man I remembered. He had broken capillaries on his nose and a tooth missing up front.

"So, you're driving now," he said.

"Have been for a while."

"Dan tells me Duke Wayne is working on helicopters in Iraq."

"He's National Guard. Should be working state side but they sent him over anyway."

"Leave it to Uncle Sam to rewrite the rules. He's a strong kid. He'll make it through. Heidi ever come back this way?"

"No. Ever hear from her after that night?" I asked.

"Never did. Me and Winona are just passing through, thought we'd say hi. Her dad is sick so we're heading up north, see him one last time."

I wanted to say something meaningful, but nothing came to mind.

"Well," he said, pushing back his chair and standing. "Looks like I've taken up most of your afternoon." He held out his hand and Dan shook it.

"You and Winona are welcome to bed down here for the night," said Dan.

"Thanks anyway, but I think we'd better hit the road, catch a trucker going north." He turned to me and patted my shoulder. "I'll write when we get settled somewheres." I nodded. I knew he wouldn't and he knew I knew. It's just one of those things you say to fill an awkward void. Without a word I wrapped my arms around his thin shoulders, that man in the boots and the button-fly jeans with the Camels tucked in his sleeve. I smelled the smoke in his hair, the whiskey on his breath and managed to

hold back my tears.

"Have a safe trip, Gaylord."

He held me at arms' length.

"You're a right pretty girl, Bossy."

I watched from the porch as he and the Shoshone woman gathered up their things and walked down the driveway toward the highway. A few years later I heard he died of a stroke somewhere in north Idaho.

Duke Wayne came home on furlough a couple times. He looked older and war-weary. He still had nightmares and woke in a sweat, but I couldn't tell if they were about the past or the war. On his third tour of duty, the boy who was named after a movie cowboy, returned home in a flag-draped box. Dan took his old suit out of the closet and buried his boy. He handled his loss with stoic grace but he was never quite the same.

The third day of the roundup was unseasonably hot.

"When you saddle Navajo would you toss a saddle on Buckwheat?" asked Dan. I felt the earth shift slightly on its axis. Dan had saddled his own horse since he was old enough to climb from a fence rail into the saddle.

"Sure thing," I said. "You go finish your coffee."

He patted me on the shoulder. "You been my right hand, Bossy."

That night after a long day in the saddle, Dan went to bed and didn't wake up in the morning. Dr. Moss said he'd been keeping his prostate cancer secret for about nine months.

* * * * * * *

A few days later I sat across the kitchen table from our family lawyer, Gordon Benchley. "I'm going to skip over all the legalese," he said, "and get down to brass tacks. The bank account, the C.D., the ranch and everything in it goes to his biological daughter."

"Biological daughter? He never married. I didn't think he had any kids."

"He never married because his daughter's mother was already married to someone else. He left it all to Evangeline Draper. That's you, my dear."

A moment of stunned silence followed.

"I'm confused," I said. "You mean Heidi's brother, my uncle, is my father?"

"He's not Heidi's brother. Heidi is a Haversham. Didn't you know that?"

"I never heard that name before."

"Well, it's a fact. Dan and Heidi got together for a brief period of time when Gaylord was carrying on with that waitress from the Silver Spur."

"That's a lot to swallow in one bite, Mr. Benchley."

"Well, this should make it go down easier," he said, turning back to the will.

That evening I cried as I went through the documents in the attic trunk. I found the photo of my great-great grandmother, Evangeline Harper Wellstone, the lady who homesteaded this land. When I got around to changing my name in front of Judge Tenacre it was not to Cheyenne or Turquoise. I became Evangeline Wellstone, the person I was always meant to be.

* * * * * * *

The next spring found me digging a garden patch behind the barn while the earth was still soft from the winter rains. I turned over the sandy soil one shovel-full at a time, taking in the scent of the warm earth, tossing aside buried bottles and rusty cans.

About fifteen inches down I unearthed a slender chain caked with dirt. I tossed the shovel aside, bent over and gave it a gentle pull. There was a slight tug of resistance before it surrendered. The chain was attached to something that almost fell apart in my hands. I brushed it off with my finger tips. It was the sorry remnant of a silver fish scale purse, fragile with rot. I turned it over, a million buried memories rushing back. The burns. The belt. The bottle of gin exploding against the side of Jason's

patrol car and Heidi banging her head against the window as the neighbor's cheered and clapped.

I leaned against the barn to catch my breath and remembered the day that Dan told us he'd killed a rattler behind the barn. I tossed the purse aside, grabbed the shovel and kept digging. This time the slender heel of a lady's shoe poked to the surface.

I tried to feel something, anything, for the woman who'd carried that purse and worn that shoe and bought a bottle of gin and a blonde wig on the day before she died. Maybe someday I'll evoke a tender thought or produce a single tear, but today is not that day.

I could have dug deeper but I didn't. Perhaps the earth has a right to the secrets it keeps. I re-interred the purse and the shoe and tamped down the soil with my boot.

I already knew all I needed to know.

ANGEL DOLL

I step off of the Greyhound Bus into the midnight rain. I'm wearing my one good pair of shoes, a decent suit beneath my trench coat and a brown fedora pulled low on my forehead. My leather suitcase carries the sum of my worldly possessions and tucked into my wallet is the paltry remainder of the fifty bucks Aunt Pearl bestowed upon me, provided I seek my fortune elsewhere.

Well, Santa Paulina, is about as 'elsewhere' as one can get from the stiff front parlors of Boston. I set my suitcase on the sidewalk and pull up my collar but the rain is already drizzling down my back. If this is an example of sunny California, I wonder what it's like on a bad day.

I head down Cork Street toward The Rexford Hotel where my old war buddy, Hank Featherstone, is holding a job for me. It won't pay what my cop salary had, but, I can drink on the job provided I don't get as soused as I was the day I was allowed to resign from The Force. When I asked Hank what my duties entailed, he simply said, "keeping the lid on things." I'm better at that than keeping the cork in the bottle, so I accept the offer.

I'm half way to my destination when an icy headwind gets the best of me and I duck through the first unlocked door I come to. I find myself standing in The Blue Rose Dancehall...a classy euphemism for Dime A-Dance Joint.

Couples are slow-dancing under a revolving mirror ball that throws dizzying arrows of light around the room. In the dark corners, pocket flasks catch the light. Prohibition has lost favor,

even among the tight-lipped Bible thumpers that crammed it down our throats, so nobody's all that worried about getting busted. You'd think the building was on fire for all the cigarette smoke. I inhale deeply and cough. Just my kind of place.

I check my things at the counter and spring for ten dance tickets like I can afford to blow a buck. I sit on a bench along the wall to dry off and size up the place. Soldiers, laborers, thugs, grifters, and farm boys straight from the Dust Bowl, circle the floor with ladies wearing too much make-up and too many artificial flowers in their hair. Beneath the testosterone and cheap after-shave is the undercurrent of lonely desperation. But hell, it's 1933. Everybody's on the skids except Al Capone.

I can't take my eyes off the pretty girl in the blue dress. She has a heart-shaped face and a mouth like the pink lipstick kiss on a love letter. The problem is, the jug-earred loser she's dancing with is holding her so tight she can't breathe. She struggles and panics. He laughs and tightens his grip.

I forget about firing up my Lucky and walk over. The guy's drunk. I can see he's not the kind you can reason with so I knock him cold right out of the chute. I'm not the young gladiator I was when I joined The Force, but my fist is still a cinder block, A couple cheerful young soldiers scrape him off the floor and toss him into the rain.

Now the girl is with me. She looks too young to be out after dark. She's even forgotten the heavy make-up and fake flowers. I ask her if she's okay. She wipes away a frightened tear and nods.

"I'm Jack Dunning," I say.

"Angel Dahl," she says, but I take it for Doll, like if she uses her real name, some maniac might look her up in the phone book. I hand her a dance ticket and she settles in my arms like a soft little kitten. Then she tenses and I feel resistance along her spine.

"It's not what you think," I say. "It's just my gun."

She blushes. Her complexion is delicate and pale like a hothouse flower.

"Your gun?" she says.

"I was fifteen years on The Force. I'm naked without it."

"I saw the suitcase. Are you coming or going?"

"I'm four days out of Boston. I'll be working security at The Rexford."

"That's where I live. Maybe we could walk together after I get off."

"Sure," I say."

The top of her head fits beneath my chin. Her hair smells like roses. We dance slow and sensuous to Stormy Weather and a jazz rendition of The Shadow Waltz. I drown in the scent of her and the knots at my center unravel.

The lights flick on and off and it's closing time.

We walk toward The Rexford. I carry my suitcase, my other arm around Angel's shoulders. No woman should walk alone on a night like this. The rain sounds like buckshot on the canopy of her umbrella. A flash of lightning. Thunder crackles and snaps like a frayed electrical cable.

We start across the alley between Sal's Pawn Shop and The Rescue Mission when the goddamn Blarney Stone lands in the center of my back. I cave, fall to one knee, nearly paralyzed by the blow, my suitcase skidding across the sidewalk. I should be paying attention to my surroundings instead of thinking about the girl, how pretty she is, how good she smells.

Angel screams and her umbrella flies off in the wind. I struggle to my feet, pain radiating from my lumbar into my left leg. Jug-ears stands there grinning, swinging a sock that appears loaded with billiard balls. His breath is eighty proof. A match flame and the whole block would be gone.

I grab my suitcase so when he goes at me a second time I have a shield. He wields the balls like a medieval mace and leaves big dents in the leather. I can go for my gun, but blowing away a local on my first night in Santa Paulina might make a bad first impression.

Angel sees the patrol car before I do and flags it down. The officer bolts from the car, handcuffs at the ready, rain filling the

brim of his cap. He's big, red Irish with more than a drop of the old Viking blood.

"Drop the weapon like a good fellow, Elmer," he says, like it's not the first time he's dealt with the miscreant. "I'll give you a nice dry place to sleep it off."

The cop wears heavy gloves and he drops the cuffs. He bends to pick them up and Elmer winds up for a head shot. I step in and snatch away the weapon before it picks up momentum. Red straightens up, walks up to the offender. "That wasn't very nice," he says, and lands a good one to the solar plexus. Elmer's wind abandons his chest with a noisy honk. His eyes roll into his head and he drops like a stone. Red flicks his eyes in my direction.

"Grab an arm." We dump him against the wall of the pawn shop beneath a striped awning. Red reaches out to shake my hand but my back seizes. I stumble into him and he feels the gun. We size each other up and sense a primal bond, like a wolf when he recognizes a member of his own pack.

"You okay?" he asks. He has blue eyes and pale, sun-sensitive skin.

"He got me a good one," I say, tossing the weapon on the pawn shop roof. "I'll be all right after a hot bath and a good night's sleep." I extend my hand and this time we connect.

"I appreciate your help. I'm Jim Tunney, S.P.P.D."

"Jack Dunning, B.P.D., retired."

He gives me a quizzical look. "Bakersfield?"

I laugh. "Boston." Angel's beside me again, her hand in the crook of my elbow.

"I thought you talked funny," he says, good-naturedly. "You could have plugged that guy, but you didn't."

"No, but someone will sooner or later. Why rob them of the pleasure?"

"Good point. You must be Hank's new security guy."

"That I am. Word sure gets around."

"No secrets in Little Ireland. Come on you two, get in. He can sleep it off where he is." I grab my suitcase. The umbrella's

somewhere in Timbuktu.

We cross Dublin and Kildare Streets and he drops us off in front of The Rexford. We agree to get together for a drink once I'm settled in. I sense the change in Angel Doll the minute we walk into the lobby of the hotel. A man seated in a chair against the wall looks at her over his racing form with eyes as hard and cold as bullets. Except for a white tie and hatband he's dressed completely in black. He has sharp high cheekbones and there's not enough fat on his body to grease a frying pan. Angel's eyes reflect both fear and defiance.

"Angel?" I say.

Without a word she pulls away from me and takes the elevator to the second floor.. The guy favors me with a victorious smirk. I figure I've got plenty of time to knock it off his kisser so I let it ride.

The lobby looks like a million lobbies in a million towns. It has comfortable leather chairs on an oriental carpet decorated with the requisite number of cigarette burns. There's a scattering of potted palms, tables for magazines and newspapers and several art deco sand buckets bristling with cigarette butts.

The men who sit in the chairs look like a million men in a million towns. There may be a few female residents but the lobby is obviously a male domain. I see washed-up boxers, race track devotees, factory workers and pensioners of mild demeanor who probably went bust in '29.

Hank looks up from behind the reception counter and his face lights up. He's older and grayer than the last time I saw him. I walk over and slap him on the shoulder.

"You old son-of-gun," I say. "Looks like you've done okay for yourself."

"It's not The Ritz, but it keeps me in brandy and cigars."

My back cramps and I lean my elbows on the counter. "Some crazy son of-a-bitch blind-sided me with a sock filled with billiard balls."

"That would be Elmer Ganguzza. He's the town nut. I can have Doc McBane here in ten minutes."

"Let's see how I feel in the morning. Right now I'm beat."

"Well, you're a few days early. How about you relax over the weekend and start on Monday?"

"Sounds like a plan. By the way, who's the mortician with the racing form?" I look over my shoulder. The racing form sits on an empty chair.

"Axel Teague. As soon as you walked away he followed the girl up the elevator. I'd watch your back around him if I were you."

Hank opens a desk drawer. I recognize the envelope he hands me. It's my termination check from The Department. I rip it open. It's not like I've won The Irish Sweepstakes but it's enough to keep the wolf from the door until payday at The Rexford.

"Want me to cash it?" asks Hank

"Sure thing." I sign the back and he doles out the cash.

"If you want to keep your life uncomplicated, I'd think twice about the girl," he says. "Teague gets a little touchy."

"Thanks for the heads up," I say. But I don't want to think. I don't want to change her, figure her out or psychoanalyze her. I want to hold her close and slow dance in the dark with my eyes closed. Hell with Teague.

My key goes to a corner room with a small private bathroom. The neon marquee from the movie theater across Cork Street bounces ripples of color from the asphalt onto my ceiling. After I loosen my muscles with a hot shower, I wrap a towel around my hips. I head for the bed, when there's a knock on the door.

Angel says, "Jack, it's me." I open the door. She comes in and I lock it behind her. There's a fresh bruise on her cheekbone.

"Teague?" I say. She nods.

"What's his hold on you?" I examine the bruise and she winces.

"When my parents died I was thirteen. Teague showed up out of nowhere, said he was a distant uncle. I went with him because I had nowhere else to go. By the time I realized what he wanted me for I was trapped. Without me and a few of the girls

from The Blue Rose, he'd have to get a job. You're a nice man, Jack. You deserve to know the score.

"We're going to get to the bottom of this right now. I'm going to start by kicking the living shit out of the creep.

"He won't be back until Monday when he's gambled his money away."

She turns toward the door. "I have to go. If I don't meet my quota there'll be hell to pay when he gets back." The windowpane rattled in the rising wind.

I hold the door closed. "Wait, just wait a minute." I remove one of the larger bills from my wallet and slip it into her beaded purse. "You're not going out in the rain. I'll see to it you don't have to do this anymore."

She turns to me and begins unbuttoning her dress.

"No, this isn't...," and I begin to fasten the buttons.

She presses her fingers to my lips. "Don't say a word, Jack."

The dress slides off of her shoulders to the floor. Another subtle shrug and she's wrapped in nothing but the pale translucence of her skin. She reaches out and pulls the towel from my hips, takes my hand and pushes me back on the bed. A tremor runs the length of my body. Her perfumed hair falls over my face, her breasts warm and firm against my chest. She's far too young or I'm far too old, however you want to look at it, but the urge is too strong and I haven't been with anyone since.... A painful lump forms in my throat. I take my hands and press downward on her hips. She gives a sharp cry and I moan deep in my throat.

Her soft, full lips find mine but when I close my eyes it's another time, another place...even another woman. I try to get her out of my head, but Sandra slips between us like a ghost, I'm twenty three again and she's sixteen. We make love on a hillside with fireworks exploding in the midnight sky. She was my first true love and she loved me more than a' bum like me deserved to be loved...until I ruined it all.

Suddenly, I'm back in the room over-looking Cork Street. I roll over and Angel is beneath me. Be here now, I tell myself.

Be alive in this moment. I immerse myself in Angel, intensely and completely.

Afterward I light two Lucky's and watch the streams of purple smoke dissolve in the semi-darkness. Lightning flickers and thunder rolls across the roof. Angel turns on her side, one hand in my hair, the other holding her cigarette.

"Are you married?" she asks. I hear the rain ticking against the windowpane.

"Divorced."

"Did you cheat on her?" Just a question. No judgment in her voice.

"Only with Jack Daniels," I say. She looks into my eyes, senses my pain and ambivalence.

"I think you're still married in your head," she says and kisses me softly on the temple.

I wake to a gray morning. Angel's gone back to her room. A wound is always more painful on the second day and my back is proof positive. It takes me five minutes to get out of bed and straighten up. I soak in the tub. My muscles loosen up some, but a pinched nerve in my spine sends a shock wave down my left leg. I want another shot at Elmer Ganguzza.

It's Saturday. Angel's on the schedule at The Blue Rose tonight. I want her out of there as soon as I can came up with a plan. We want to be together but it'll never work unless we get Teague out of the picture. Hank tells me a guy like that has got to have a past...a record...a warrant...something. He shows me his rental application. His former residence was in Kansas City. The rest of the information is sketchy, deliberately evasive.

"He's just arrogant enough to use his real name," says Hank. "Might be worth checking into, weed out the riffraff."

"I know just the guy who can help me with that."

I call Jim at the precinct. He says he'll do some checking and get back to me.

Angel and I have pancakes and coffee at the Memory Lights Cafe on the corner of Cork and Dublin. She wears a blue rain-coat and matching boots, her hair long and flowing and dotted

with raindrops. I pay the check and we hurry back up the street to catch the new Jean Harlow movie.

We laugh and eat popcorn and drink Coke. Today I don't feel like a broken down cop with an ex-wife who hates him. With Angel I have a second chance to do things right, maybe even kick the booze.

The curtain comes down on the double feature. My spine is vapor locked from sitting. I suppress a groan and drag myself out of the seat. I was wrong about the broken down cop thing. I feel like a dog that's been hit by a truck.

It's after dark and we're back on the sidewalk. The flickering neon marquee turns the raindrops pink and silver. Across the street, in a recessed entryway, a couple doors down from the hotel, a ruby light glows from the shadows. It could be someone ducking out of the rain for a smoke. It could also be Teague watching us. I'd walk over and check it out if I were by myself, but Angel is chattering on about the movie, asking if she should bleach and bob her hair like a Hollywood star. Why ruin her fun by starting a ruckus?

Evening. Angel puts on a pink taffeta dress, matching shoes, and a string of dime store pearls.

"I wish you wouldn't go," I say. "Let me take care of you?"

"Oh Jack," she says. "They say you can't fall in love this fast, but...."

"What do they know?" I hold her close for a moment and kiss her cheek.

"I'll just pick up my check and say good-bye to the girls so they won't think something bad has happened to me. Then I'll call it quits."

I give her taxi money and see her off in the cab. When I return to the lobby I can still smell the ghost of her perfume.

I return to the room and the phone is ringing. Hank patches Jim Tunney through. He tells me to go in the alley entrance of the brick building next door, that it was The Zebra Room before Prohibition. Now it's the speakeasy where the cops and attorneys hang out.

I have Angel to take care of now so I can't waste all my money on booze. I leave a five in my wallet and put the rest of the bills in the top dresser drawer beside my gun. Who needs a gun? I'm having drinks with a cop who looks like a trigger-happy leprechaun.

The doorman lets me in and points to a red leather booth in a dark corner. Jim's already ordered a bucket of beer and two chilled mugs. I can tell by the look on his face that he's got something for me.

"You dug up some shit on Teague," I say.

He grins. "The deeper I dig the darker it gets."

I fill my mug. I'm thirsty as hell from all that popcorn.

"So let me have it." I lean forward on my elbows and a shard of pain shoots from my lumbar into my neck. I clench my jaw, try not to lose my focus.

"You were right about Kansas City," he says. "Seems that every hooker who wanted out of his stable ended up in the river with her hands tied behind her back. Believe me, you don't want to hear all the gruesome details."

"So, how come he's still walking around?"

"He skipped town with a couple of his girls when he became the main focus of the investigation. Need I say, he left no forwarding address?"

"Is that it?"

"Right now he's just wanted for questioning. There is, however, an outstanding bench warrant for unpaid traffic tickets."

"Unpaid traffic tickets?"

I let the thought marinate.

"Ever extradite someone to another state on a traffic charge?"

"This could be a first," he says, and laughs.

"And once he's back in Kansas City, they can grill him on the murders."

Great minds with but a single thought," he says, downing his beer in one long pull.

"Tomorrow?" I say. "It could keep a friend of mine out of the

morgue."

"Why not. Tomorrow it is."

I cross the alley to The Rexford. I'm buzzed after sharing a couple buckets of beer, my throat rough from too many cigarettes. A day in Santa Paulina and I have a job, a girl, two friends and an enemy. What more can a guy ask for?

The moment I enter the lobby I know something is off. Trouble is written all over Hank's face..

"It's Angel," he says. "She's frantic. I tried to tell her you were next door but she'd already started up the elevator. Someone knocked the hell out of her. That's the way it is with these girls."

"Oh shit! Teague," I say. "Try and catch Tunney before he leaves The Zebra Room."

I can't wait for the elevator to come back down. I hobble up stairs I'd have normally taken two at a time. I reach the second story landing, calling for Angel. I follow the trail of her rose perfume down the hall. The door to my room is open. Pearls from her necklace are scattered across the floor. The top dresser drawer is upside down on the bed. My money's gone. My gun is gone. Angel Doll is gone.

The floor vibrates beneath my feet. It's the elevator on its downward descent. I scramble down the stairs and stumble. The nerves in my back are on fire. It's all I can do to keep my bad leg under me.

Hank meets me at the bottom of the stairs.

"She jumped in a cab going west on Cork," he says.

"Any idea where she's gone?"

"If I were that scared, I'd be on the midnight train to L.A. It's the first place Teague will look for her."

Hank rushes across the room and reaches under the counter.

"Jack," he calls, and tosses me a set of keys. "It's the black Ford Coupe out back. Cork turns to River Road when you cross the bridge. Go another mile and turn right on Depot Street."

I gun down Cork in the midnight rain, the windshield wipers working overtime, the tires hissing over the asphalt. I fly past the Rescue Mission, the pawn shop, The Blue Rose Dancehall. I

clatter over the Santa Paulina Bridge, the water black and raging one hundred feet below. When I get to Depot I snap a right and slide up to the station.

Passengers fold their umbrellas as they file onto the train. A few turn their heads to watch the stone-faced man who's dragging the lady away from the tracks. He's left the door open and the engine running in his yellow Caddy, like this is going to be easy, like it's going to be a Sunday walk in the park. I guess it's up to me to screw up his plan. I hobble out of the car.

Angel sees me. "Jack!" she cries. "Jack!"

Teague spins around. He takes in my limp, considers me an insignificant nuisance. Maybe he's right. I look like a wounded animal.

"Get lost," he says. "I have legal custody of this little tramp."

Angel struggles to free her wrist. Her hair is tangled over one eye. It looks like spun gold in the light from the station. Her coat is torn. One of her earrings is missing.

The station master pokes his head out of the office door.

"We got trouble here, mister?"

"Call the precinct," I say. "This man is wanted for murder." He disappears inside the building.

Teague snorts in disgust.

"I'm not wanted for shit," he says.

I'm not in fighting form. If Hank connects with Officer Tunney, he could be here any second. If he doesn't, it will take the city cops a minimum of ten minutes to get here. I stall. I have to use my head. I limp to the Caddy. I reach in, turn off the engine and toss the keys into the darkness. Teague's confidence goes down a notch. Angel swings with her free hand and hits him in the head with her purse. His hat tumbles off and he drops her wrist.

I power-limp across the platform but Teague's bunched fist has already connected with Angel's cheekbone. She staggers sideways and loses a pink shoe. I can't think my way out of this one. I land a good one on Teague's jaw. Something cracks...a tooth...maybe a bone. I'm unable to strut like a horny rooster,

but there's nothing wrong with my fist.

"You son-of-a-bitch:" he says. His hard-soled shoe slams into my ribs. I feel the cartilage rip and a bolt of lightning explodes in my back.

A switchblade flicks open in his hand. My back clenches and in that brief moment of paralysis I know he's got me. I hear a siren in the distance but it's too late. Teague gives me a broken-toothed smile. I have no choice but to make a final play and go for the knife. I grab for his wrist as he aims for my gut. Angel screams.

A bullet whines past my ear and I duck. The knife clatters to the planks. Teague needs both hands to plug the hole in his throat, but he's sprung a sizeable leak and blood dribbles from between his fingers. Surprise and disbelief register on his face. He's wondering how such a sterling fellow as himself can come to such a gruesome end. He drops to his knees with a gurgle, falls flat on his face and bleeds out on the boards.

Angel stands over him with my gun in her hand. Her eye is swollen closed. Blood is dripping from deep inside one ear.

"Hand me the gun," I say. "It's all right. Everything is going to be all right." She's shell-shocked. I don't think she hears me. I take a step toward her and she takes a step back. The train whistle blows. The train begins to move slowly down the tracks. Angel looks at me, then at the train, then at me with an expression of utter terror and helplessness. "Angel," I say, "trust me," but she's slipped into a dead zone beyond my orbit.

Angel turns and drops the gun. She runs along the platform as the train picks up speed. I start after her, but my leg buckles and I go down. She raises her arm above her head. The conductor reaches down and pulls her aboard. My last vision of Angel Doll is her tear-stained face at the train window, her little hand pressed against the glass.

Someone pulls me to my feet. It's Jim. He strides over .to the body and pockets the gun. A second patrol car pulls up and two officers get out. Jim addresses the younger of the two.

"Duggan, would you see that the black Ford gets back to

Hank Feather stone at The Rexford? This gentleman is too injured to drive."

"Yessir," he says, and heads for the car.

"Boyle, forget the ambulance and get the coroner down here."

"Right away, sir. Do you know who did this?"

"Mr. Dunning seems to be the only witness. I'll see what he has to say."

"Who's the victim?"

"There is no victim. The deceased is Axel Teague."

Boyle scratches his head. "If there's no victim, there's no perp."

"You get smarter every day, Boyle," he says and bags the blade.

Jim stops the car on the bridge. The night is pitch black and the river is roaring. He takes my gun out of his pocket and tosses it over the railing. "So there won't be any questions later," he says. "Got a problem with that?" I shake my head. "The way I see it...no girl...no gun...no sweat."

"That's the way I'd tell it," I say.

We drive in silence for awhile with the rain pounding down.

"Jack," he says. "A word of advice. Don't obsess over the girl. Sure, you could follow her to L.A., but believe me, by the time you find her, she won't be alone."

"Aren't you a little ray of sunshine," I say.

He sputters a laugh. There's a trace of a smile on my lips as he turns the windshield wipers on high. We pass the Blue Rose Dancehall. The door swings open and Elmer Ganguzza sails through the air and lands chin first on the sidewalk.

"Jesus," I say. "Boston or Santa Paulina, some things never change."

"No shit. Speaking of Boston, ever work cold cases?"

"I've worked my share."

"The Chief wonders if you'd consider working a few of ours. It shouldn't interfere with what you've got going at The Rexford and a guy can always use a couple extra bucks."

For a second or two I vacillate between the truth and an out

and out whopper.

Then I say, "Before I sign on, you should know they canned my butt in Boston because I drink too much. I'm still on the bottle."

He grinned.

"Then you and the Chief should hit it off just fine."

Three A.M. back at The Rexford and Hank calls in the doc.

"Nobody on the second floor can sleep with all that moaning," he says.

The doc shoots me in the hip with a needle the size of a rolling pin and the pain melts away like warm candle wax.

Alone in my room I down a shot of Jack Daniels and savor the mellow burn. I listen to the rain tick against the window-pane and watch the reflections of neon light ripple across the ceiling. I've had one hell of a welcome to my new town.

I light the last Lucky in the pack and think of Angel and how her pale velvet skin felt against mine. I think of her soft hair against my cheek and the intoxicating waves of rose perfume. One glorious night together and what do I have to show for it? A broken string of dime store pearls and an empty wallet. It's not that funny, but I can't help smiling.

"They say you can't fall in love this fast," said Angel Doll. Maybe not, but what we had was a damn good facsimile. She couldn't take the place of Sandra...no one could...but, she was one hell of a quick fix for a lonely guy with a bum leg.

Angel Doll is getting off the train in downtown L.A. about now. She'll be wearing a torn blue raincoat and one pink shoe. She'll have enough money for a little food and a week or two in a hotel, provided it's near the Greyhound Station and she doesn't mind sharing the bathroom down the hall with washed up hookers and derelicts. Then again, with her angel face, she might nail a rich guy or a married businessman who can afford to keep a woman on the side. I wonder where she'll be in a month or a year. I wonder if she will ever think of me.

FAMILY MYTHOLOGY

My boyhood hero was my Uncle Mick,
who joined the Force and swung a mighty stick,
and slipped me smokes behind the backyard shed,
caught thieves and murderers and shot them dead,
to spare the honest citizens the pain,
or trials, acquittals, catching them again.
He gave us rascals all his pocket change,
and took us big shots to the shooting range.
Of course the barroom beer was free at night,
for cops who kept the city running right.
Hell's meanest 'mutha' couldn't make him blink,
but Irish music made him cry, I think.
He must have been the biggest, toughest one,
to chew them bullets when he ate that gun.

ABOUT THE AUTHOR

ARLETTE LEES began her writing career several decades ago in the Confession Market and has since found a permanent home in pulp fiction.

She is a regular contributor to HARDBOILED magazine, edited by pulp fiction veteran, Gary Lovisi. One of her hair-raising tales appears in the anthology DEADLY DAMES from Bold Venture Press and a story with a real knock-out punch is included in the anthology BATTLING BOXING STORIES. BLOOD BAYOU, her twisted tale of passion and murder in the Louisiana swamp appears in WHODUNIT from WILDSIDE PRESS and takes another bow in these pages.

Arlette writes from northern California on a typewriter that is older than many of her readers. She is also an award-winning poet who is widely published both here and abroad.

"The Lees Sisters, Lonni and Arlette, are unique; these two gals write their own work in their own way, but they always deliver sharp, exciting, intense crime stories you can really sink your teeth into. You can't go wrong with the stories in this book!"

Gary Lovisi, Editor, *Hardboiled*

"If I didn't know the Lees Sisters were chicks, I would think they were hard-drinking, gun-toting vigilantes from Brooklyn. Genius, pure genius, runs in the Lees gene pool."

Cindy Rosmus, Editor, *Yellow Mama*